JENNA STARLY

AUTUMN SKY

A
Lake Lyla
ROMANCE

Also By Jenna Starly

Summer Sky

Winter Sky

Contents

"We make a living by what we get, but we make a life by what we give."
Winston Churchill

Ren C.
5th Grade Science Report
21 Years Ago

If I had to pick a planet to be, I'd pick the sun. It is over 100 times the diameter of earth and the core temperature is 27 million degrees! Technically, the sun (and the moon too) is not a planet since it does not orbit around another sun. Technically, it's a star because its gases have helium and hydrogen. Still, I'd pick it. It has tons of gravity, which holds the whole solar system together! Every other planet orbits the sun so it's fine all on its own.

Autumn

Diary Entry, Age 11

15 Years Ago

Today Bonnie Haller said Which one are you? when we were paired for badminton in PE. I hate that! Me and Bonnie just did that project together in social studies. I mean, Winter isn't even in our homeroom. When Winter when she gets home I'll tell her and she'll know what I mean.

Autumn

Diary Entry, Age 16

10 Years Ago

I'm beginning to really dislike Luke D.! I mean, he's cute and all. I get why Winter likes him. But does she have to spend SO much time with him? Yesterday, she missed our regular Gossip Girl watch party AGAIN. I asked Summer if she wanted to watch with me but she had plans with Jules. Then I overheard Winter on the phone telling LUKE all the drama that happened between three other girls in our friend group. So now she's downloading everything with HIM? He can't understand her the way I do. I know I sound bratty and I hate that. I mean, I should be happy for her because she's liked him for SO long and he's nice to her. But I thought I was Winter's ride or die. And if I'm not hers anymore, then who is mine?

Chapter 1

AUTUMN

"You've got a date."

I'm barely in the door and I'm already confused.

"A da—? What?" I take a seat and untwirl the scarf from my neck and lay it over the back of my chair. It's early September but it already feels like deep fall. There's a low-lying fog outside and a chill in the air right outside Bernie's, my favorite coffee shop here in Lake Lyla. I brush the wind-swept hair from my forehead and remove my glasses so I can rub moisture off the lenses with the hem of my sweater. "Back up, girl," I instruct.

My best friend Greta takes a deep breath both to prepare to exhale her flurry of words and also, clearly, to prevent herself from critiquing my apparent thick-headedness.

"You, Autumn Sky, have a date with a dude."

I return my eyeglasses to my nose and raise my eyebrows as if to say, *Continue, because I still don't get it*. If anyone knows that for the first time since puberty, I have absolutely zero interest in dating right now, it's Greta.

1

She grows a tad sheepish. "Weeellll, I signed you up for a dating service – a very *special* dating service – and I've found you a great guy."

Just then, Bernadette, the owner of Bernie's, arrives at our table with two mugs of espresso, steam swirling above the rims. She's a few years older than us, around 30, and her curly blond hair, with its fun streaks of blue and pink, is mostly covered by a black beanie.

"Autumn, Greta, let me know what you think," Bernadette says. "I'm experimenting with recipes for upcoming fall specials."

Greta and I are such frequent customers that Bernadette often tests her rotating door of new seasonal concoctions on us. Lavender tea lattes in March, cold brews with coconut milk in June. She usually hits the mark but trusts us to give constructive critiques. I pick up the warm ceramic mug, which fits perfectly between my palms, and inhale the scent before taking a tablespoon-sized sip. It warms me from the tip of my toes covered in hand-knit socks to my head.

"Mmmm," I say. "Do I detect hints of cinnamon? Or, wait, is it nutmeg?"

Bernadette smiles and points her finger at me, indicating that I nailed it.

"Thanks, Bern," Greta says and then returns her gaze to me. "He's a Virgo and let me tell you, you won't find any two signs more devoted to each other than Virgo and Taurus. Virgos are practical, loyal. And they can be much more flexible than you stubborn Tauruses. Both earth signs."

Astrology isn't my thing — it's Greta's. But I never yuck her yum. After all, who am I to declare that the cosmos can't sway love lives?

"So," Greta continues, "want to hear about him?"

"Do I want to hear about the guy I'm allegedly going on a date with, something that I have sub zero interest in doing?"

Despite my sarcasm, I can't really blame Greta. I've only recently announced my commitment to being independent and uncoupled for the first time in my life. After Will, my most recent boyfriend, and I broke up right before the start of summer, it occurred to me that I've never been on my own, never truly been independent. Literally never – not even before I was born.

I'm a triplet and have always had my sisters, Summer and Winter, with me. Plus, Winter and I are identical and, as a result, have an especially intense bond. I'm so conditioned to being one of (at least) a pair that even when I went away to college – we three attended different universities – I found myself moving from romantic relationship to romantic relationship with basically no meaningful time on my own. In other words, I'm a textbook serial monogamist. I've always had — let's face it, always *needed* — someone by my side. Sister, boyfriend.

Being a triplet comes with lifelong triangulation, which, I noticed a few months ago, has a similar ring to it as "strangulation." And Winter, my identical sister, and I have that extra...something that comes with sharing all of our DNA, that unspoken telepathy typical for identical twins. I know when she's coming down with a cold, even if we're hundreds of miles apart. Having her close — literally or figuratively — gives me unparalleled comfort. When she began dating Luke, her first boyfriend in high school, spending lunches, nights and weekends with him, I felt utterly lost, adrift. Without her constantly near, I didn't know who I was. Summer, being the non-identical triplet, had already separated, spending most of her free time with her best friend Jules. So I couldn't turn to her. My grades suffered. Life felt gloomy.

So what did *I* do? I got myself a boyfriend of my own because I needed *someone* by my side. That pattern continued until just a few months ago when Will and I broke up. And it really was a pattern. Looking back on all of my relationships, it was like I had a boyfriend cookie cutter. They're always tall (the taller the better) and athletic. Bonus points for tattoos. Right after Will and I broke up (triggered, like many breakups before, by the fact that I was simply too reliant on the relationship), I decided that perhaps it was finally time for me to live life individually and unpartnered for the very first time in more than 25 years.

I need to get to know myself. Do I really like science fiction movies or do I see every new release because it's Winter's favorite genre? Would I turn on an NBA game if I was home alone — or do I call myself a basketball fan because my last several boyfriends have been?

"You haven't gone on a date since May," Greta continues. "I know your work has been crazy busy the last few months...."

I'm the senior associate at Lake Lyla's tourism board. Aside from four years of college, I've lived my whole life here in Lake Lyla, the mountain lake town at the intersection of California, Oregon and Nevada that my great-great-great grandmother, Lyla Lansberg, founded in the late 1800s. My mother's family has been here for generations. So promoting tourism and assisting thousands upon thousands of visitors here with accommodations and activities is both second nature and fun for me. Though Lake Lyla is a year-round destination — with world-class skiing in the winter and a postcard-worthy fall and spring wedding setting — summer is indeed my busiest time at work.

But this summer was also consumed with something I do to keep busy when I'm not dating: helping people. For as little as

I feel I truly know myself, I *am* certain of my life motto: Add Value.

It doesn't matter if it's raising money for firefighter bonuses or rolling up my sleeves to help lay concrete for a Habitat for Humanity build, helping people is how I spend the bulk of my free time. As a poster in my office declares, "To whom much is given, much is required."

But it's more than a moral requirement — it's my lifeblood. My mom jokes that my greatest need is helping people in need. She was tickled when I pledged DG in college since one of her nicknames for me has long been "Do Gooder," and "Do Good" is Delta Gamma's nationwide slogan. My mom also sometimes called me "Mitzi" after the Yiddish word "mitzvah," which means good deed.

So working at the tourism board is perfect — guiding visitors to the wonders of Lake Lyla is something I can do in my sleep. And the predictable, limited 9-to-5 hours enable me to spend nights and weekends on these kind of passion projects. Right now, I'm collecting donations for Ukrainian refugees, planning a spaghetti feast fundraiser for a family needing financial assistance with medical care, and drafting a culturally sensitive land acknowledgment for the former Native American property the tourism board building sits on.

"So," Greta says, "I created a profile for you on Billionaire Rendezvous dot—"

"—wait! *What?*"

Again, that impish face. I can read Greta almost as well as I can read Winter.

"It's a, uh, website to match people with rich men and women."

I gag on my nutmeg espresso, drips going up my nose and down my chin. I grab a napkin and pinch my nostrils.

"*Excuse* me?"

5

"Yeah. I read about it in a magazine and it sounded amazing. Very niche. You don't have to *be* a billionaire to register, you just have to be open to dating one. I figured, why not sign you up?"

"Why not sign *you* up!"

The couple seated at the next table abruptly halts their conversation to look over at us. I give them a *nothing-to-see-here* smile and lean forward.

"Margaret," I say between gritted teeth, using her given name, the one that her mother used whenever she was in trouble as a kid. "What. Did. You. Do?"

"I figured you could be our guinea pig."

I've seen this movie before. Since the third grade, I've been Greta's guinea pig for anything she wants to test out. When we were in middle school, she convinced *me* to attempt the raw jalapeño pepper challenge first. In high school, she signed us up for auditions for the spring play but put my name on the try-out spot forty-five minutes before hers.

"You mean if this God-forsaken 'match' turns out to be a disaster — which, by the way, it most certainly will — then you can watch me suffer the consequences from a distance?"

"No, no! I just figured that between the two of us, you — with your pretty face and generous, bubbly personality — would be the most likely to have success. And then if it works for you, I'll dive in next!"

I lean back. "Let's just assume I accept your ridiculous premise," I begin, implying that I do not. Greta is tall, voluptuous, smart and hilarious and therefore just as likely to have success on this site — or any dating app — as anyone. "Why would you create a profile for me on a site for *billionaires* of all things? I'm so not a billionaire, so not a billionaire's type, and not even remotely impressed with billionaires. They are...how do I put this...*gross*. Amoral sharks. Greedy, heartless workaholics –"

"*You're* a workaholic."

She's not wrong. She's not referring to my job at the tourism board, but rather to my never-ending parade of volunteer projects, which keep me constantly occupied. I've taken on even more projects in recent months in my deliberate effort to finally live life as a singleton. By extension, my charity work keeps Greta busy too because I rope her into helping whenever I find myself in over my head with fundraisers and donation drives. She's a dog groomer and, at my urging, has groomed countless stray, shelter and foster dogs for free. And I regularly twist her arm into fostering needy dogs and cats since my own apartment building prohibits pets.

I place my palms on the table, close my eyes and take a deep breath. It's no use arguing with Greta's description of me as a workaholic because it's true.

"Billionaires aren't special. Any one of us here could be wealthy," I say, gesturing around Bernie's as a way to represent the population of Lake Lyla as a whole. "We're smart enough, ambitious enough. But we've made different choices. We're not money hungry."

"It'll be just like Pretty Woman," she adds ignoring my point just as deftly as I ignored hers. "You know, the gorgeous woman and the billionaire, both who need love...."

As Greta well knows, Pretty Woman is my all-time favorite movie, my comfort watch. I've seen it thirty-six times and counting. I've listened to podcasts analyzing its symbolism, read blogs dissecting its social commentary. Obviously, Greta had at the ready counter arguments to all of my objections to this ridiculous idea because of course she did. Next to my triplet sisters, she knows me better than anyone.

I flash her my right palm. "Don't try to convince me with Pretty Woman. While I cannot deny its profound entertainment value, I object to the twisted sexual politics of the arrangement. Billionaire Edward Lewis is condescending and Vivian Ward does *not* need to be saved."

"Don't you want to at least see his *picture*? Read the man's profile? He sounds pretty special." She waves a printout. "He's really something else."

Even though I've pledged myself to an indeterminate period of independence, I *am* a little curious. Who wouldn't be? Plus, at least one of the reasons I've always been in constant relationships is that I love men. I love the way they smell, I love their broad shoulders, their deep voices and—.

"Too busy," I finally say, stopping myself before I get carried away. "I've got Summer's wedding and the spaghetti fundraiser coming up. And there was that hurricane in the Gulf Coast last week so funds will be needed for victims there and—"

Greta smiles, shaking her head slowly. "Autie, that won't fly with me. You're never *too* busy. As your sisters and I have long joked, you should have been named *Spring* given your abundance of energy. I even put that in your Billionaire Rendezvous profile!"

I sigh and glance around the coffee shop, taking in the scene. The snap and roar of the fireplace in the corner, Bernadette behind the counter with all kinds of ingredients – maple syrup, cinnamon, chocolate shavings – before her. Tourists and Lake Lylans seated at the tables around us, leather boots on their feet and puffy vests covering their torsos.

Summer's wedding *is* coming up in a few weeks. I could not be more excited for her — she and Cole are beyond perfect for each other and she's so in love. And I *have* had a hard time convincing her and Winter that I don't need a plus-one to the wedding given my commitment to being solo for the foreseeable future. I considered bringing someone, anyone, just to placate them, to get them to stop asking about it. But all my guy friends are in relationships. Asking Noah, my closest friend at work, was tempting. He's exactly the kind of man I go for: 6'1", plays basketball in his free time. That's the problem, though. Not only could it be awkward work-wise, but Noah is exactly the kind of man I always go for, always seem to need. Bringing him would not exactly be breaking the lifelong cycle of co-dependency I'm determined to break.

But Greta's nudging, her interference in my love life *does* give me an idea. Perhaps if someone like this guy, someone I can *pretend* is my date, is on the wedding guest list, my sisters will stop badgering me. And then I can stay focused on my personal projects, like helping Ukrainian refugees, among others.

I point to the paper profile Greta is swinging in front of me like a hypnotist's watch. "Let me see that."

Chapter 2

REN

"I've got the Stableton Incorporated contract for your review, the Muir Steele purchase waiting for your signature. The CEO of Stardragon is on hold and the plane is being sanitized as we speak."

My assistant Leah is standing at my desk placing files and papers before me as she lists items that need my attention or signature. She's framed by the enormous window overlooking the San Francisco Bay, the nearby hills and water gleaming with a distinct Mediterranean feel. All too familiar with my impatience and withering attention span, her sentences are efficient and factual. Leah has worked with me for more than a decade. Long before becoming my assistant, she was my friend, my best friend since sixth grade. She's been keeping me on task and helping curb my nerdy tendencies since we were eleven. I sometimes wonder how I'd get through life without her. I'm the pitcher to her catcher — I get the glory but she makes the calls. Then again, Leah would be the first to insist that ours is a mutually beneficial relationship. In addition to giving her this well-compensated job that she loves and excels at, I also introduced Leah to her wife Samantha, the only thing or person she loves more than her job.

"Ren," she says, tapping her index finger on the stack before me and then snapping her fingers, "keep up." She sounds just like she did when we were in high school and she had to yank me from my "just one more level" obsession with whatever video game I was playing so that we could cram for the AP History exam. (Thanks solely to her, we both aced it.)

I sign Warren T. Castillo on the first three documents.

"One last thing," she says, "I've narrowed down the women from Billionaire Rendezvous dot com."

I resisted — just short of refused — Leah's insistence that I bring a date to the upcoming Infinity Symposium, the year's most important conference for space entrepreneurs. I'm not one for dating in general, having long grown comfortable being single. Not only am I an only child, but I was raised primarily by my grandmother, who took care of me while my mom and dad, a management consultant and securities lawyer, were hyper-focused on their careers.

My own workaholic tendencies are clearly inherited. The son of immigrants, my dad grew up fearing that he'd be underestimated because of his last name. Determined to exceed expectations, he attended the best schools, always graduating at the top of his class. He landed prestigious summer internships, spent a year clerking for a federal court judge, then was the youngest person to become partner at a premiere securities law firm. He never explicitly pressured me to achieve the great heights he did, but I, too, had the last name that ignorant bigots might use to undervalue me. Meanwhile, my mother's parents grew up in a time when there were quotas for people like her — in schools, in jobs. So like my dad, my mom understood that she had to work doubly hard to prove her value.

I'm beyond proud of their hustle and what they've achieved. But both my parents move through life like they're making up for something, proving something. And by fulfilling their professional goals, they sacrificed time with their only child. They still work tons and, ironically, don't really even spend their money. At least I *enjoy* my fortune.

I grew up spending time alone and as an adult, I prefer it. Achieving success in my industry — space — I have everything I need. A chef cooks healthy, flavorful meals, with a large focus on Asian and Italian cuisines, my favorites. A fitness trainer arrives to my home in San Francisco's Pacific Heights neighborhood three times a week and works me out in my full gym and then I get to recover in my infrared sauna. Chefs, trainers and others are on standby when I'm at my other homes in Seattle, Los Angeles and other cities where I frequently travel for business. A private plane takes me wherever I need — or am in the mood — to go. I have unlimited funds to purchase one-of-a-kind maps and get one-on-one input from world class experts in cartography, one of my personal passions. My San Francisco home even has a ballroom where I can bring in entertainers to perform for me and friends. And I have...

Leah snaps her fingers.

...an assistant who organizes my life.

"So there's this one," she says, pointing to a file, which has paper clipped to the top a professional photo of a woman who, while attractive, has an aggressive, come-hither look. "And this one." She plunks down another file and photo, this one of a woman who reminds me of a friend in college who used to kick my ass in Dungeons and Dragons. "And this one." The final file has a clearly candid photo of a woman caught mid-laugh, her smile wide. She's wearing a slouchy cowl around her neck, which frames her delicate face. "This last one," Leah adds, "has the distinct advantage of living in the precise location of the conference."

Leah finally convinced me to bring a date to the Infinity Symposium, where this year I'll be the keynote speaker. She's sure that having a date will deter the normal barrage of colleagues and acquaintances trying to not-so-subtly set me up with their sisters, friends, daughters, nieces, mail carriers, etc. I'm under no illusions that these Victorian era attempts at matchmaking are about me. Being a lifelong geek, I fully grasp that I'm "desirable" solely due to my billionaire status.

And I get it. I, too, am driven largely by money. Why would I blame someone else for the same?

But it's embarrassing and tiresome being a 30-something single billionaire, the focus of celebrity watchers. Someone even set up an Instagram account devoted to my love life called "Courting Castillo." It has 55,000 followers.

Sixth-grade Ren wants to crawl into a hole sometimes.

The Infinity Symposium is a cannot-be-missed summit for the elite movers and shakers in the space industry. The highest level women and men in space law, space art, private and commercial space exploration, among other specialties, congregate to share ideas, make deals, reveal constantly emerging technology, and more. There will be scientists, entrepreneurs and academics.

Leah and I are acutely aware: *I must be at the top of my game all four days.*

Immediately after all obligatory events, I must retreat to my private suite to over-prepare for the next day of moderating panels. I might have just enough time for an evening shower and maybe a few reruns of The Simpsons before crashing and getting up the next morning to do it all over again. Captive in a small mountain lake town for four days, I cannot waste one iota of energy making small talk or hearing why I just "have to meet" someone's female friend or relative.

At last year's Infinity Symposium, an aging engineer whose company I was eager to acquire asked me to dinner, which I agreed to even though it meant missing an evening program on solar physics that I'd long been looking forward to. When I arrived at the hotel restaurant, I discovered that he'd brought along his daughter. Instead of discussing share prices and strategic corporate planning, I had to listen to him drone on about her stints as a model and social media influencer. After thirty minutes, he claimed to not feel well and excused himself, along with a "you two kids stay and get to know each other better" command. His daughter was boring and bored, and I spent the rest of the dinner supremely aggravated that I missed the presentation on space plasma.

So Leah and I decided that this year, especially as keynote speaker, I need a stand-in, a decoy, someone who will keep at bay anyone on the hunt for a rich, single man. In the old days, Leah would simply pose as my girlfriend, a practice that started with junior prom when neither of us had dates of our own — me, because I was dorky, and Leah, because the girl she had a crush on was dating some lacrosse bro. But Leah's marriage to Samantha two years ago was highlighted in "Courting Castillo," instantly dispelling the longtime rumor that Leah was my romantic partner. So she can't sub in.

"What do *you* think?" I ask Leah about the Billionaire Rendezvous files. I have so much on my plate, including a report to review about the intersection of AI and space travel, not to mention writing a magazine opinion piece about managing big data from space-based assets. I just don't have the energy to pick among these three women who will simply serve a temporary, limited role.

"I liked this one because, like you, she's interested in wine. Plus, she kind of looks like Samantha."

"Uh, that's kind of twisted."

"Thought so too." She flips to the next file. "I picked this one because this will be a pretend relationship and she has acting experience."

Wordlessly, we bust out laughing. It's likely that *all* of these men and women with profiles on Billionaire Rendezvous are actors, whether they admit to it or not.

"Next," I say.

"And this one, in addition to living in Lake Lyla, where the Mountain Peak Inn & Resort is located, says she is known among friends for an abundance of positive energy."

I sigh. "Are we sure this is even a good idea?"

Kenny, my business advisor, was strongly against it. He's crazy conservative when it comes to anyone getting close to me — whether it's an accountant or a wine sommelier I befriend. He's sure everyone wants to scam me. But Kenny has been with me a long time. We met in college in the finance and investments club. We worked together on several campus networking events and even did a summer internship together at a Silicon Valley start-up. When my assets hit $10 million in my early twenties, it was Kenny who I called on for business advice. He's aggressive and money-driven. If Leah is my right-hand woman, then Kenny is my left-hand man.

"Maybe I should just suffer through another long weekend of people showing me photos of their daughters or the propositions of female space industry execs who want to double our fortunes through marriage?"

"No, Ren," Leah says. "We're sticking with this plan."

Maybe I should consult the person who, next to Leah, knows me best: my grandmother. But she's *also* someone who's always trying to set me up, albeit for different reasons.

A typical grandmother, she wants me to "settle down," to stop following in my parents' footsteps by working all the time, to the exclusion of a vibrant family life.

But I know myself — I'm not fit for coupledom.

Sure, I've had my share of girlfriends, both before and after I became financially successful. But no relationship lasted longer than nine or ten months. As much as I loved each woman — and I did — being part of a couple felt overwhelming, suffocating. Spending so much time with another person became...too much. And I never felt that I could truly be myself, my nerdy self, with any of the women. I'd have my cartography catalogs sent to my office. I feigned interest in the symphony when, in reality, I much preferred staying home and watching movies or old sitcoms.

"Are you sure this is the site we should use? If we're concerned about me being bombarded by gold diggers, then why are we on a site *designed* for billionaire dating?"

"Quit being cynical. Kenny's influencing you too much," she says. "If they're gold diggers, then they'll eagerly agree to a short-term arrangement that involves four days at a fancy resort known for its five-star food and its spa, even if it means sacrificing long-term love."

I yawn. I really don't have the energy for this. "Okay, okay, I trust you."

"Of course you do."

"So who to pick?"

Leah furrows her brow dramatically as if she's truly contemplating the choice. But I know that she zeroed in on the person long before bringing me these files and that showing me three files instead of just one is her way of creating the illusion that I have a choice. I love her for it.

From the gold-plated dispenser at the side of my desk, I pump a little hand sanitizer into my palms as I wait for her

17

to "think." When the viscous clear liquid is rubbed in and dried, I follow it with a pump of hand lotion from a matching dispenser.

"Did you say the CEO of Stardragon was on hold?" I ask.

"Yeah, he can wait."

She moves one file to the right and then hovers an index finger over the remaining two, like a silent eeny-mee-ny-miny-moe.

Finally, she presses her finger down on the candid photo of the woman from Lake Lyla. "This one."

Chapter 3

AUTUMN

Once, when I was 17, I went to the grocery store by myself. It was my dad's birthday and Summer, Winter and I planned to make his favorite dessert: caramel bread pudding. I was assigned to go shopping for the ingredients.

It was a rare moment that I enjoyed being by myself. I'd just gotten my driver's license and I felt so grown up pushing the cart down the aisle, filling it with items like all-purpose flour and vanilla extract after comparing prices and selecting the best values. After gathering everything, plus a box of raspberry Pop Tarts just for me, I got in line for check-out.

There were two carts ahead of me. First in line, loading the rest of her items, was the mom of one of my classmates. She took note of me, waved, and said, "Always a treat to see one of the Sky sisters." (I was pretty sure she said that because she didn't know if I was Autumn or Winter.) Behind her was a couple in their 20's who were clearly tourists. It was late May and they had a basket, rather than a cart, filled with simple things like pasta, wine, cereal, milk and graham crackers, chocolate bars and marshmallows for s'mores. As I waited my turn, I skimmed a People displayed on the magazine rack.

When it was the couple's turn to move up, the woman's flip-flop made an odd noise as she walked, and I noticed then that she sort of dragged one foot as she moved. I took a closer look and saw for the first time that the woman was wearing sunglasses — indoors. Her face was caked with foundation.

I replaced the People on the rack and moved my cart forward, keeping my eye on the couple. Something felt off about them — the way the man spoke to the cashier in brusque, one-word sentences, the way the woman didn't speak at all, the way he handed *her* the single bag to carry when they were done, the way she trailed behind him with that leg dragging.

I put my few ingredients on the conveyer belt, still keeping my eye on the couple, trying to sort out what was gnawing at me. As the woman turned the corner to exit the sliding glass doors I spotted a fading, green-ish bruise on the back of the woman's thigh.

It was in the shape of a hand.

The blood left my skull. I froze in place.

Suddenly I knew exactly what was wrong but I didn't know what to do. Should I tell the cashier, who was distracted by an item whose wrinkled package wasn't scanning? Should I call 911?

I wished I wasn't alone. I wished I was with my mom or at the very least my sisters. Winter would definitely know what to do.

"Miss?" The cashier was extending her arm, holding a receipt and two printed coupons that the machine had spit out.

Jolted from my panic, I paid, grabbed the receipt and my bag and ran out the same door the couple had exited.

Once outside, I surveyed the parking lot, searching for the couple. Nothing. Then I heard the screech of tires and saw a car pull out of the lot, turning right onto the main road. A second after that, they were gone. I hadn't even been able to register if the car was black or blue.

The woman — her listless walk, her defeated body posture, her efforts to cover (almost all of) her bruises — haunted me for days. I replayed the two-minute scene over and over, wondering what I could have done differently, how I could have protected or saved the woman. I wondered whether she'd already been beaten again — or worse.

Finally, I couldn't take it anymore. I decided that if I couldn't help her, I could help women *like* her. I researched county services for domestic violence survivors and found an organization that needed volunteers. It was my doorway into the world of volunteering, of helping, of giving back beyond school bake sales and other small-scale help I'd given before that. Initially, I did administrative chores for the organization, like stuffing and stamping fundraising letters. Then I assisted the event coordinator with tasks — calling vendors, creating seating arrangements — related to the organization's upcoming fundraiser. After a few months, I was allowed to start answering phones. Every time I spoke to a caller about how we could help, I pictured the woman from the supermarket.

That tiny moment in time affected my life forever. I gained so much from volunteering with that domestic violence organization. Not just practical skills like making spreadsheets and soft skills like how to work with colleagues, but I also experienced deep personal fulfillment by spending my free time improving someone else's life.

Yet that also created a bit of a conundrum of conscience, one that was crystalized for me, by, of all things, Joey and Phoebe on Friends. In the episode featuring a PBS telethon, Joey insists to Phoebe that *selfless* good deeds don't exist. It got me thinking.

Was I volunteering because it made me feel less guilty about failing to help the woman in the grocery store? Was I helping because it made *me* feel good?

In the end, as I took on more and more volunteer projects for organizations with different missions, I decided it didn't matter. Whatever my motivation or the side benefit of feeling good about myself, helping others was still worthwhile. It made me feel connected to the world — and that was especially important then because that's when I was feeling my connection to Winter, my identical sister, slowly diminish. To this day, I'm happiest when busying myself by doing something for others.

To help with the conscience conundrum, I kept my work at the domestic violence organization private. I didn't even mention it on my college applications. And it was then I adopted my "Add Value" personal motto.

I still wonder about that woman, though.

"Oooh, try this."

Winter hands me a slice. We're with Summer at the Lake Lyla Apple Festival, a Labor Day weekend tradition we've been coming to since we were five months old, according to our parents.

I take the piece of apple from her. Its skin is smooth and its flesh a creamy white. I bite into it and its sweet and tangy juices coat my tongue.

"Delicious," I say.

"Well, if you like the Honeycrisp, then give this one a try," says the man at the stall as he holds out a plate with more slices fanned out attractively. These apples are yellowish green on the outside and have a pinkish hue inside. Summer, Winter and I each take a sample. This one is tart and less juicy but still tasty.

The man explains that there are more than 2,500 varieties of apples. "And now the third in this 'flight' is an Ambrosia."

We pinch the last slices and are about to bite into them.

"Wait, wait!" The man lifts up a jar of honey. "Dip the end in here before you taste. The sweetness of the honey perfectly balances the floral notes of this variety."

"Apples and honey – just like on Rosh Hashanah," Summer says.

We dip as we're told.

"This one's my favorite," I say, covering my mouth as I chew. "Sweet. Extra crisp."

"Mine too," the man says.

We say our thank yous and continue walking around the festival, which is on the grounds of the Moonlight Peak Inn & Resort, a 150-acre property known by Lake Lyla locals as simply the Inn. It's the site of everything from celebrity weddings to fancy golf tournaments to many of the community fundraisers I've organized over the years. The perfect mix of luxury and rustic, casual comfort, the grounds are spectacular this time of year. The Inn is nestled just high enough amidst the mountains for the lake to be visible over the tops of the Douglas firs and big-leaf maples. Today, on the Sunday of Labor Day weekend, the colors are otherworldly. It's a stunning mixture of rust and burnt yellow from the trees, browns and grays from the mountains, and the bright blue of the lake, which is framed in white as wind creates tiny waves at its edges.

We move along to the next stall, maple and oak leaves crunching underneath our feet. We sample apple cider and taste various apple sauces mixed with other fruits such as raspberries and end-of-summer peaches.

"So, ladies, which is your favorite?" the woman minding the stand asks.

"This one," Summer says, pointing to the applesauce with berries.

"I like this one," Winter and I say simultaneously as we point to the exact same sample of cider, the one made from Braeburn apples.

"Well," the woman says, "seeing as you two are *clearly* twins, I'm not surprised you preferred the same."

I'm not surprised either. Much to my chagrin, I should add. Most people, like this woman, assume that Summer is merely our other sister and that Winter and I are identical twins. This has always been hard for Summer. But in recent years, I've realized that being one of the identical sisters has downsides too, at least for me. It's why I started wearing glasses even though I don't need them because my vision (like Winter's) is 20/20. But I want my own look.

Winter and I have always shared a unique bond, with classic twin clairvoyance complete with that ability to finish each other's sentences, to feel each other's pain. But it also means nonstop togetherness, even when we're apart. Much of the lore about identical sisters — unknowingly putting on the same outfits when getting dressed miles apart, getting the exact same questions right and wrong on standardized tests — is true. And it's probably because of these things that even when I'm not with Winter, I feel an inexplicable longing, a need to connect, to attach myself to something or someone beyond myself. My whole life, I've felt...incomplete, ungrounded whenever I'm not paired, whether with Winter or, later, a romantic partner. I'm not one for one night stands. I prefer deep relationships. And I've never been single for more than a few months.

A college friend who studied psychology said my obvious need to recreate the close twin bond in my romantic relationships meant I'd forever feel frustrated. At first, I dismissed her theories, insisting that I simply like men, like being part of a couple. And that's true — it's wonderful to have someone to check in with in the morning, at night and in the middle of the day. To say simply, "Hey" when a boyfriend picks up the phone. I like being someone's priority and having someone else as mine.

But after Will and I broke up in May, I finally began to wonder if my friend was right. It's definitely not healthy that being away from a boyfriend even for a few hours sometimes made me feel ill. Maybe my romantic relationships never turned into something lasting because I have to first truly experience life as a singleton. Once that notion arose, my conviction grew: I *had* to create my own sense of self. If not now, in my mid-20's, then when?

Winter slips her arm through mine and guides the three of us to the next stall, a bakery with all sorts of apple-based items, including apple bread pudding, apple cookies, miniature apple pies, even apple brownies. A breeze picks up and blows several brown square napkins off the table. I lean down to retrieve them and notice the spider webs that have formed between the legs of the table, their intricate patterns glistening in the late afternoon September sun. A bluebird hops nearby searching for wayward crumbs. I hand the napkins to the baker and cross my arms across my chest, rubbing my palms along opposite shoulders, the sleeves of my flannel shirt soft underneath.

We spend a few minutes gorging on baked goods and visiting with old high school friends that we run into at the next stall, some still locals, some visiting family for the long weekend. Then the three of us decide, mutely, to meander along the backside of the Inn, away from the Apple Festival. There's a small creek that runs parallel to the back of the 100-room hotel, a spot we loved as kids. For a time, our uncle was a manager at the Inn and sometimes our parents would help him out during big events. The three of us, and our little brother Colin, would play along this creek while they worked.

We settle on the familiar large boulders along the bank and sit side by side by side looking at the water. Like the nearby Fallon River, the creek is markedly shallower than it was when we were kids, thanks to climate change.

"I'm stuffed," Winter says.

Me too, I think, both amazed and not at all amazed that I was just about to utter those very same words.

"Sum, how are wedding plans going?" I say instead.

Summer met Cole, the love of her life, several months ago, and they're getting married soon. He and his daughter Livvy are a fantastic addition to our family. Summer has blossomed in the last months, finally overcoming the trauma of a past relationship. She also started a new job working with middle schoolers that has proven to be the perfect match for her skills and talents. Her happiness is infectious.

"Flowers are picked and the invitations are done. Now we're focused on planning the reception and finding a photographer. So overall, we're on track. Speaking of that, Autie, who should we add as your plus-one on the invitation?"

Here we go.

"I told you, I'm happy to go solo."

"Come on," Winter says, "I'm bringing a date so you should too."

"You're bringing a *friend*," I counter.

"So? It's gonna seriously throw off the photos if you don't have a date."

"Can't you bring a friend too?" Summer says.

I could, of course. I still wonder if I should ask Noah from work. He's good-looking, smart, a hard worker. Since he started working at the tourism board earlier this year, he's become my closest friend in the office. In recent weeks, we've started getting mid-afternoon frozen yogurts together on Fridays. He started bingeing Downton Abbey at my suggestion and he introduced me to his favorite TV show Castle, which I'm now obsessed with. He even helped me restring my guitar when I bought it used a few months ago. But even just considering Noah for my date feels too habitual, too comfortable because he's so much like other guys I've dated: tall, sporty, funny. And I promised myself I'd diverge from the well-worn path of being paired, of having the emotional safety of a companion.

I roll my hands into gentle fists. *It's time to challenge myself, to see who I can be other than a triplet, somebody's identical sister or someone's girlfriend.*

The creek dribbles. A noisy sparrow chirps at a nearby finch. A rabbit dashes from right to left across the bank. A damp smell is what remains from the earlier morning fog that's finally lifted.

"Did I tell you guys about the spaghetti feed fundraiser I'm working on? It's going to raise money for—"

"Don't try to change the subject," Summer says, her blue eyes shining, an aura of warmth and peace around her face.

God, I'm happy for my sister's happiness.

"I can't explain it," Summer adds, "but it would just make me so happy if the three of us were there together and all matched up. Three pairs."

Crap.

There's nothing I wouldn't do for my sisters, but I also want to be true to myself. Maybe Greta's sneaky plan with that ridiculous billionaire website is the way to go. Maybe I can meet with this guy a couple of times, just long enough to bring him to Summer's wedding. I didn't admit it out loud to Greta but Ren Castillo *was* handsome. I barely skimmed his profile, but going on looks alone, he'd look spectacular in the wedding photos — even if years from now Summer's kids will look at those pictures and ask, "Who the heck was that guy with Auntie Aut?"

I breathe in the cold, clean air and return Summer's affable, open gaze. "Okay, okay. *Maybe* I'll bring someone. But I'm deciding who. Stay tuned."

Chapter 4

REN

"How's it going, Matthew?"

"Very well, Mr. Castillo."

I stare pointedly at my driver and he course corrects. It's been three years but I still have to insist.

"Right, right. *Ren*. I'm doing fine, Ren. Thank you."

Matthew slides open the long paneled door to the van that serves as my personalized mobile workspace. A former ride-share driver, Matthew takes me everywhere from Silicon Valley to Lake Tahoe. After a single Uber ride three years ago with Matthew, a driver who skillfully wended his way through Financial District traffic and got me to the airport with unexpected time to spare, I offered him — on the spot — a position driving exclusively for me.

"To the Prius dealership, Mr.— Ren?"

"Yep. Jordan Boulevard in San Rafael."

I settle myself into the van I had custom built a few years ago. It enables me to do things like make calls to space commodification and navigation specialists and study up on advances on aerospace engineering, all while traveling between in-person meetings. It's a smaller version of the plane I also designed. Here, in the van, there's a table with a couch on one side and desk chair on the other so I can work from different vantage points. There's also a small bathroom with a shower and toilet and a short galley kitchen with a microwave, fridge and espresso maker. Right now, we're headed about 15 miles north of San Francisco so I can pick up my new car, an all-electric vehicle I can use whenever I'm in the mood to drive myself.

Given my work in the space industry, I've come to understand the dire nature of climate change and how chlorine and bromine molecules cause ozone depletion. So I do everything I can to minimize my own carbon footprint. Hence, the electric vehicle. A Tesla seemed too flashy, too cliché for someone like me. So I went with a Prius. And even this van is a plug-in hybrid, one of the very few ever produced.

"All settled?" Matthew calls from the front seat.

"Good to go."

I pull out my iPad and review an agreement for my auction purchase of a 1789 map of North America. Although I have plenty of work to do, including an investment opportunity in a nano-satellite manufacturing company and a review of the prototype of a debris-collision detector one of my companies is developing, it's Labor Day weekend. So I've blocked out the day to handle personal business like picking up my new car and hitting "add to cart" on two other antique maps. I will turn to work this evening, as I do most nights, weekend or not. My grandmother will likely call me this evening, as she does frequently, to implore me to get out and have some fun, to go find myself "a nice girl" instead of focusing on business all the time.

My grandmother is more responsible for my upbringing than my parents, who were busy making their way to the pinnacle of their respective professions. It was hard — and often lonely — growing up playing second fiddle to their careers. But I'm grateful they modeled a strong work ethic. My grandmother — my mother's mother — lived with us from the time I was born. Given that I'm an only child, she and I spent lots of quality time together. When I was old enough, she introduced me to Cheers and The Simpsons. A game lover, she taught me to play Hearts and Canasta. Wednesday evenings she'd have her best girlfriends over for their weekly "mah jongg and margaritas" gathering. I'd fall asleep those nights to the joyful sounds of them laughing and calling out words like "one bam" and "three dot" amidst the roar of the Osterizer as they made more drinks.

My grandmother even spurred my interest in maps. It was a hobby pursued by my grandfather, her husband who died before I was born. One evening, when I was about eight, she pulled from our attic some of his old maps, including a pull-down school map of Cold War Communist Russia from the 1950s and a worldwide pictorial map from the 1960s, and let me hang them in my room. I loved the detail, the purely visual representation of information, the way the images told a story of the time. I studied them for hours. Given my success in the corporate space industry, I've been able to pursue this passion in earnest, acquiring the rarest of maps and meeting other collectors as well as world-class cartographers.

Out the van's window facing east, I see Matthew's now reached the Golden Gate Bridge, the one-mile, rust-colored suspension bridge connecting San Francisco and Marin County. Hovering over the intersection of the San Francisco Bay and the Pacific Ocean, I spot Alcatraz and then Angel Island, once the point of entry for West Coast immigrants and now a historic state park accessible by ferry. My Eastern European ancestors came to the US in the early 20th century via the East Coast equivalent, Ellis Island. My Latin ancestors crossed the southern border.

It's a perfect September day, fall supplying some of the warmest days of the year in the Bay Area. Sailboats dot the bay and surfers catch moderate waves on the southern side of the bridge.

I've come to love how this van cocoons me even though we're traveling on the very edge of the country, the gateway to the Pacific. We cross completely over to the Marin County side and enter the famous rainbow tunnel. I silently hold my breath as my grandmother and I used to do whenever we traveled through tunnels when I was a kid.

We crest the hill above Sausalito and begin a downward descent. I turn to glance out the west-facing window and notice a tall Taco Bell sign just off the highway. It's then I realize I haven't eaten breakfast yet, something that would surprise my grandmother because she knows I love a good breakfast, particularly her legendary from-scratch blintzes with blueberry sauce.

I twist my wrist to glance at my Rolex. It's 11:30.

"Matthew," I say, leaning towards to the driver's seat, "mind pulling over at the next exit and doubling back to that Taco Bell back there?"

"Sure thing."

My weight shifts forward as Matthew expertly maneuvers the van across several freeway lanes to take the next exit. A few minutes later, we pull into the Taco Bell parking lot.

"What would you like?" Matthew asks, unbuckling.

"No, no. I'm getting it. What would *you* like?"

"Oh, no, I couldn't –"

"Matthew. Knock it off. It's fast freakin' food."

He looks both chagrined and pleased. "Nachos?"

"Good choice."

Just outside the restaurant, a woman who looks not much older than me sits next to a large, sad-eyed dog and holds a handwritten sign that says simply, "Hungry."

I pat the seat of my pants in search of my wallet, then remember it's in my jacket. I pull it out, pinch a $100 bill from the stack, and place it in the bucket she's positioned at the sleeping dog's nose.

A few minutes later, I'm back in the van with Matthew's nachos as well as a spicy breakfast burrito and bag of cinnamon twists for me. I open the small fridge and pour myself the tiniest splash of red wine. There's just something about burritos mixed with the acidic mouth feel of red wine that I've come to love. Wine is another one of my hobbies, this one a newer interest I discovered after sitting next to a wine lawyer at a fancy gala. I normally hate those events, the gratuitous speakers and the live auctions. I'm all for supporting good causes. But I've come to prefer just sending a check unless there's a particularly interesting speaker on the agenda. At that particular event, the lawyer had recently earned his sommelier certification as a way to enhance his law practice and we got into a fascinating discussion about the subtleties of wine pairings and the latest developments in bottle storage. After that night, I decided to learn a little about wines myself by reading specialty magazines and hiring a sommelier to give me a crash course on up-and-coming wine regions (and then buying and studying maps of vineyards in those areas). And though not technically a space-related investment, I did help fund a Sonoma start-up developing technology to determine the optimal time to pick grapes given the climate change's impact on a millennia-old practice. And not long after my initial deep dive into wine, I somehow stumbled upon this tasty, high-low burrito-merlot combo.

Matthew crunches up the bag his nachos came in and takes a swig from his water bottle. "Thanks, Ren. Hit the spot."

"No sweat," I say, my mouth full of a greasy cinnamon twist.

"Remain here or get back on the road?"

"Go on ahead."

Matthew starts up the engine and we resume our drive to the car dealership. I chase my two small sips of merlot with several gulps of water and then return my attention to new additions to my favorite online map catalog. The van now reeks of hot sauce and chilies and I'm not mad about it.

A text dings from Leah, who reminds me to log onto Billionaire Rendezvous to formally begin the conversation with the woman I hope will agree to be my date to the Infinity Symposium. To my frustration, Leah is leaving me on my own here. She was my Cyrano during high school and beyond, helping me draft emails and texts to whatever woman I had a crush on at that time. But for some reason, once she narrowed down the women on this site, she's taken a hands-off approach. I consider texting her back asking what, exactly, I should say in my message. But then I hear in my head the voice of my grandmother, who reminds me I'm over 30, a "big boy" who shouldn't rely on "underlings" to do everything for me.

I laugh a little to myself. Practical and down-to-earth, my grandmother is decidedly unimpressed with my success as a space entrepreneur. I've tried to buy her things — new cars, new clothes — but she declines. She cares little about money, focusing more on whether I'm a mensch, a person of integrity and honor, the kind of person who helps others without any expectation of payback, the kind of person who knows right from wrong and never crosses the line. I wonder if this woman – Autumn is apparently her name – will even read my message, let alone accept an invitation to video chat.

But if she does and if all goes well, I will ask her to be my date for the four-day work conference.

Normally, I can rely at least a little on the fact that I'm, well, rich, as that will usually ensure at least one date even if I might otherwise be considered a little too...boring or geeky. But given that the whole damn site is designed for billionaire dating, I'm no one special in this case. I look again at her photo. Her large, light brown eyes shimmer even through her stylish glasses. Her broad smile exudes a brightness, a happy energy. I expect nothing short of rejection.

I look up from my iPad and stare once again out the window, now seeing Tiburon, with its picturesque coves and small marina, pass by in the distance. Though I still feel like the 15-year-old nerd I once was, I gather my resolve.

"Well," I whisper, placing my fingers on the screen ready to type, "here goes nothing."

Chapter 5

REN

"Ready for your Meet Cute?" Leah says as she barges into my office and switches on the massive TV screen mounted on the wall.

"My what?"

"When two characters in a rom com meet for the first time, it's called the Meet Cute."

"What's a rom com?" I say, elongating my words to further fake my ignorance.

Leah rolls her eyes. Together, we've watched more than our fair share of classic rom coms over the years — Pretty Woman, You've Got Mail, Can't Buy Me Love. She even introduced me to rom com books and I'm not ashamed to admit I dive into them once in a while when I need a break from mergers and acquisitions reports and white papers from scientific foundations.

"F off, Ren. Ready for your video chat? Fix your collar. It's crooked and makes you look like a shlump."

"Truer words from the hero's sidekick have never been spoken."

Leah flicks her thumb and index finger at me like I'm an unwanted bug crawling up her forearm.

It's the Tuesday after Labor Day. I spent the bulk of the holiday weekend reading academic journals about ethical colonization through space transport, reviewing the work of up-and-coming space artists, and taking my new carbon-neutral car out for a spin. I drove from my Pacific Heights home twenty miles south into Pacifica on the coast. I bought a slice of pepperoni pizza and watched hard-core surfers catch massive waves. I tested out the sound system, blasting Dave Matthews Band on the way there and back. It wasn't your typical Labor Day barbecue or luxurious end-of-summer beach day, but it suited me just fine.

Now I'm back in my 20th floor office, with its modern, minimalist furniture and chrome finishes. Some might say my office is too clinical, but to me its sparseness is comforting, familiar. Still, even the clean lines of my surroundings don't sooth my nerves, which are slightly rattled by this impending call with a potential date from Billionaire Rendezvous. I remind myself that this office, this TV screen is where I've solidified deals that have made me millions of dollars in a single afternoon. I close my eyes, trying to summon that commanding, confident energy I feel when running my business and apply it to my imminent Meet Cute. (What a dumb name — there's a verb or an adjective missing from that expression.)

As Leah dials in, my cell phone buzzes with a call from my business advisor Kenny. I don't pick up. Moments later, the office phone begins its incessant ringing.

"Hey," Leah says while adjusting the computer's camera, "shut off those calls, will ya?"

"Who is whose assistant anyway?"

Leah snorts as I silence both my cell and office phones. But the calls are a reminder that I *do* need to zero in on a contract for low-methane rocket fuel and finalize the charter for a new school for space aviation pilots, not to mention draft speeches for the very conference for which I need a companion in the first place. But for the next few minutes at least, I commit to securing a date so that when the conference rolls around I'm actually able to maintain my focus on the substantive programs and on making business connections rather than fending off proposals to be set up.

Leah finishes setting up the video and sits in a chair just outside the camera's view.

"Can you please join me here?" I ask, nodding to the empty seat next to me.

"Really, Ren? On your first meeting with this woman?"

"Yes, really," I say, pointing forcefully to the chair. "I want expectations to be clear. We're proposing not a love match but a *business* relationship solely for the duration of the Infinity Symposium. Having my trusty assistant beside me will reinforce that."

"Whatever you say," Leah says halfheartedly as she moves into the seat. She takes a sip of her drink. I wrinkle my nose as soon as I catch a whiff.

"Really, Leah? Pumpkin spice lattes already? It's barely September and in San Francisco anyway, it's still peak summer weather. I'm still drinking these," I say, lifting a cold brew coffee and jiggling the ice around.

"Pumpkin spice lattes — my beloved PSLs — just landed on the menu two days ago. This fall, I pledge to have one every single day until they're replaced with peppermint lattes in December."

I shrug. "You do you."

The screen begins blooming to life as my potential date is signing on. I hear her voice before the video appears. "You promise, it's just temporary, right?"

"Yes!" says another voice. "Now you're on."

Suddenly, the face of the woman named Autumn appears on the screen. She's even prettier than her photo. Her cheekbones are sculpted and her skin is rosy. Her teeth are large with pleasing curved edges. Her hair is swept into a high, messy bun and she's wearing stylish eyeglasses. Her arms are waving beneath the screen as if she's shooing someone else out of the frame. Her own wing woman, perhaps.

"Just temporary, huh?" I say in what I think is a lighthearted tone. But Leah gives me a withered look that says, *Not a great opener, bud.*

"Uh, well, yes. Hi, I'm Autumn." She flattens her hands to the side of her head to tame the small hairs that have escaped her bun. Her smile is broad, friendly.

"Ren." I point to my chest. *Dork*, I think.

"I've, uh, got to be honest...." Autumn begins.

Her tone implies she's going to end the call right away, to call the whole thing – whatever this is – off. Three minutes ago, I would have been relieved. But now that I've seen her, heard her voice, part of me is disappointed.

"...this whole thing wasn't exactly my idea," she continues.

"To be frank, Autumn," I say, leaning forward as if to confide a secret, "it wasn't mine either." I glance at Leah and point my thumb at her. "This is my assistant, Leah. The mastermind."

The women give each other brief, genial waves. Then Autumn grabs the arm of the person she shooed away and now pulls her in front of the camera.

"Well, while we're making introductions, you might as well meet Greta. She signed me up for this...whatever *this* is, without my knowledge. Wrote my profile and everything."

I look down at the printout Leah had placed on the table before the call. I lift the paper and read from it. "So does that mean you're *not* 'generous, energetic, a do-er'?"

Autumn looks at her friend with the expression of someone who's been complimented by a person whose opinion means a lot. Then she looks back at me. "Greta wrote that, but I suppose it's a fair description."

"It's a very accurate description, if I do say so myself," Greta says, leaning sideways so I can see her in the screen. "She's a Taurus, you know. That means that you, as a Virgo — your birthday is in your profile — should have a harmonious energy with Autumn. I'm guessing you're hard working..."

Leah dips her chin and raises her eyebrows in silent confirmation.

"...and as Autumn's longtime best friend, I can assure you that she's got all the best qualities of a Taurus: also hard-working as well as determined and honest."

"So if your friend arranged this, why are you here, Autumn?" I ask, moving my hand in front of me to indicate "here" means this unusual, get-to-know-you video call. I ignore the Virgo-Taurus connection because although I've centered my adult life on the cosmos, that hasn't included astrology.

"Why are *you* here?" she responds with a smile.

Fair enough.

Leah jumps in. "Given the site on which Greta and I connected you two, you obviously know that Ren here is a very wealthy man. As a result, he's the subject of much speculation and the object of...desire for many people who want to set him up with their friends, their family members. Not just set them up on a date but set them up *for life*, so to speak."

Autumn laughs, circling a stray hair around so it settles behind her ear. "I'll bet."

"Mr. Castillo has an important, multi-day conference coming up. Right in your town, as a matter of fact. He's the keynote speaker and has a big role to play."

"Can't get distracted," I add.

41

Autumn nods. "I can imagine." She gently pushes Greta back to her original spot outside the frame. "So you need a...decoy? Someone to serve as your date so fellow attendees won't derail you from the business tasks at hand?"

"Exactly," Leah and I say in unison.

"Well, that's actually a relief to hear because, as you heard me say as we logged on, I, too, need a temporary...let's say, stand-in...for an upcoming event. My sister's wedding is coming up very soon, also here in Lake Lyla, and I need to bring someone."

"No one there for you to bring?" I ask.

She shakes her head and sits up straighter. "For a variety of reasons, I am quite committed to an extended period of not dating."

I push my lower lip up towards my upper lip and nod. *I get it.*

"Sounds like you two have a mutual interest in an artificial relationship," Leah says. "Why don't you chat to see if it'll be a good fit? I'll be right next door in my office. Nice to meet you Autumn. You too, Greta, wherever you are."

Greta darts one hand in front of the camera and waves.

"Your assistant has her own office? In San Francisco, where commercial rent is higher than London, than Manhattan, than Tokyo?"

"She deserves it." I don't reveal that I'm considering purchasing the entire building. "So let's take her advice: tell me about yourself. What do you do?"

"Clearly nothing as lucrative as what you do. Don't even have my own office, let alone an assistant who has one too. I'm a senior associate at the Lake Lyla tourism board. I help visitors to the area arrange everything from adventure travel to lodging. I draft advertising campaigns to attract tourists. I do market research and work with local officials on all things tourism related."

"Sounds interesting."

"Interesting enough. More importantly, it leaves me lots of time for other activities."

"Such as?"

She shrugs. "Hobbies? Tried a pottery class — turns out it wasn't for me. But I recently picked up guitar. So far, I've learned Brown Eyed Girl and Stand by Me. But my real passion is helping others. Collecting donations for needy people or animals, planning fundraisers. Stuff like that. How about you? Dated a lot?"

"Wow, really diving right in."

She blushes.

"No, it's okay. I like it – you're direct. I've had a few serious relationships over the years. But I confess I don't date much these days. Too swamped with work."

"What do you do, exactly?"

"I'm a space entrepreneur."

"A what?"

I love this question because I get to geek out. "Historically, space exploration has been under the purview of national governments. But in recent years, interest in outer space has become privatized and—"

Suddenly the chair beneath me wiggles inexplicably. I inhale sharply, wondering if perhaps I drank too much cold brew this morning.

But then my center of gravity sways, and the floor-to-ceiling windows jiggle in their frames. Leah bursts back into my office, looking frantic, her PSL spilling onto her wrists as she dashes next to me, grabbing my shoulder.

On screen, Autumn bolts upright and blinks rapidly. Her jaw hinges open. "Ren? Leah? Everything okay?"

43

Chapter 6

AUTUMN

"Uh, we just had a small earthquake," the man named Ren says, clearly shaken but also stiffening his spine in an effort not to show it. He throws a brotherly arm around his assistant Leah, who doesn't attempt to conceal that she's completely freaked.

"Did you feel it where you are?" she spits out, breathless.

Lake Lyla is about 300 miles north of San Francisco. We occasionally feel the larger earthquakes centered in the Bay Area, often many moments after San Franciscans do. Greta and I glance at each other, wordlessly confirming that we're squarely planted on solid ground. I look back at the camera and shake my head.

"I'm guessing that was in the high threes or low fours," Ren says, referring to the Richter Scale. "Small and quick. I think it's over." He tosses Leah a reassuring look. "Remember, small quakes are good — they release built-up pressure."

His assistant exhales and then leaves the room on what look like unstable legs.

Ren claps his hands together to recenter his attention. "Apologies for that interruption."

"None needed. Earthquakes are terrifying."

"Earthquakes and wildfires: the joys of California living!"

I laugh, understanding the subtext – that despite these perennial dangers, neither of us would want to live anywhere else. "Yup, whenever an earthquake begins, you can't help but wonder, 'Is this it?' 'The Big One' we've been warned about our whole lives."

"Exactly."

"So, you were saying you're a space entrepreneur. What is that, exactly?"

His cheeks curl towards his eyes and he leans forward. "So, you know, space — the sky, the atmosphere, the planets — has traditionally been governed by international laws. It's all anchored in frameworks pulled from cooperative maritime, aviation and environmental laws. But we're not in the twentieth century anymore, right? There's cutting-edge technology, new vehicles...so much! Given this rapid development, space is no longer the sole domain of national governments. Instead, it's opening to commercial exploration by private industry. What's in development is going to make virtual reality and artificial intelligence seem like child's play."

While the content of what he's saying verges on science geek, his enthusiasm is downright...adorable. He's not at all my type. Even though he's sitting down I can tell that he's on the shorter side. He looks tidy, preppy. Great hair, though — thick and nearly black. "And how did you get interested in this? For a career, I mean."

"I've always been into maps. For my ninth birthday, I got a poster of the galaxy — kind of a map of the solar system, my first exposure to cosmography, the science of the universe. It blew my mind. I started reading everything I could about space — memoirs of astronauts, science books about the planets. Space included many of the things I had a knack for: mathematics, physics, technology, engineering, and if you go deeper, even things like poetry. In college I majored in astrophysics and minored in philosophy. Oh, man, I'm totally nerding out now. I'm sorry...."

"No, no, go on." I just didn't have the heart to halt his fervor. I was expecting this billionaire to be arrogant and out of touch. But so far, Ren was showing none of that.

"Okay, last thing — I promise," he says. "Probably the main thing I love about this emerging field: most corporations have a product to sell or, in more recent decades, they make you — the consumer — the product, with information that's sold to other corporations. But with space, at this stage anyway, the product is really just...innovation."

This whole concept is so far outside my wheelhouse, making it clearer than ever that this man and I have a grand total of nothing in common and would never have crossed paths in real life. I squeeze Greta's hand out of view of the camera on my computer, which is resting on a stack of books on a coffee table in my living room. Like me, she can barely believe what we're hearing. "I see," I say with as much gusto as I can muster, though his zeal is kind of sexy.

"Space will soon include tourism –"

I perk up.

"— as well as the extraction of minerals and other commercial activities, some of which we can't even envision yet."

"How's this all regulated?"

"Excellent question," he says, pointing at me. "No ready answers. But *that's* what makes this field so exciting! New frameworks will be needed, right? There'll be liability for injuries, environmental implications, navigation and jurisdictional issues. But most of all, there are limitless *opportunities*! Imagine space art! Advertising in the sky! For that reason, space is at the top of all corporate agendas."

"Makes sense, then, that you hit, uh, a certain financial status by focusing on this area."

Greta hisses her disapproval.

"I realize it's indelicate for me to say that," I add quickly, "but we *did* meet on a site for billionaires looking to date. And by the way, just so you know, I *never* would have visited the site of my own volition." I glare at Greta, who sticks her tongue out playfully. "To be completely honest, I've always thought that billionaires are kind of, um, let's just say...not really my type. I'm more of a nonprofit gal."

To my surprise, he laughs at the minor insult. "I get it. This whole thing," he says, waving a finger at himself and then at me, "was *Leah's* idea. Definitely not mine. But, to your point, I do take money very seriously."

I think of what could be done with a billion dollars. Access to clean water for everyone who needs it. Critical funding for research into cures for cancer and dementia. Spays and neuters for every feral cat. Now, *I* lean forward. "So do I."

We're silent and I think then that we should just sign off. He seems like a nice enough guy but I'm not sure I need a date to Summer's wedding this badly. Maybe I can just deal with the constant questions and pressure from my family or maybe suck it up and take Noah from work. But Greta waves her hand in a rolling motion. *Just keep going*, she insists.

"Um," I say, "the map in that frame behind you? It's crooked. From the earthquake."

"Oh, thanks." He stands and moves a finger gently underneath the edge of the frame to right it. I catch a glimpse of his full body. He's wearing perfectly pressed khakis, a brown leather belt, a crisp baby blue button-down. *Preppy, boring*, I think. But his lower half looks toned and when he turns back around, I notice his pecs press against his shirt.

"Pretty map," I say of the weathered paper, gold tones and what looks like engraved writing. "What is it?"

He removes it from the wall and brings it closer to the camera to show me. "Argentina, from the mid-eighteen hundreds, where my ancestors lived. Cartography, map collecting, it's a hobby." He carefully returns the frame to the wall. "That, and wine."

"Beautiful." I don't comment on his interest in wine. Not only do many wine enthusiasts strike me as elitist, but also, I don't drink.

"So," he says, sitting back down, "tell me more about you." *This is pointless, but whatever.*

"I work in Lake Lyla tourism, as I mentioned. I have two sisters and a brother. We grew up here. My parents live here still, at least when they're not traveling the world on house-sitting gigs, a side hustle they picked up during their retirement."

I feel something step on top of my feet. I look down and see Greta's foster dog, a two-pound Chihuahua I convinced her to look after until we can find him a new home. We named him Zippers. He settles onto my feet, which are covered in bulky socks hand-knit by my mom, a perfect resting spot for the tiny dog. Instantly, he begins to snore. Greta chortles because Zippers likes only about three people, one of whom is me, which is why it's been hard to find him a forever home.

"And dating?" he asks.

"What about it?"

"Do you, uh, do it?"

This guy is a little awkward. "I guess you could say I'm your classic serial monogamist. I tend to have long-term relationship after long-term relationship." I don't mention that one therapist went so far as to caution me about having an unhealthy love addiction.

"But you're not in one now?"

I shake my head. "Decided a few months ago, after my last relationship ended, that I need a break. I need to experience life separate from boyfriends, separate from my sisters."

"Your sisters?"

I lean to the left and grab the framed photo of us from my side table. I notice then how different my surroundings are from those of the stranger I'm speaking with. Whereas his office boasts sharp lines, steel and minimalist decor, my home is the opposite. My one-bedroom apartment is casual, cluttered and homey. My small living room has bright-colored throw pillows, a wall covered in tapestries and small tables brimming with framed pictures.

The photo I grab is one of my favorites from when Summer got engaged last month. We're on the Eureka Queen, a beautiful boat where Summer's fiancé proposed. The background is a bright blue and Summer's wavy hair is blowing in the wind. She's flanked by me and Winter and her smile is so pure and genuine that it makes my heart sing. I hold the photo up to my computer so Ren can see.

"Here we are."

"So you and the one on the other end are identical twins. I get it now."

I shake my head. "Triplets. But yes, Winter and I are identical."

"Autumn and Winter?"

I'm used to this. "Yes, and this is Summer," I say, pointing to her.

"And you three were born in...?"

"April."

Like most people who hear this, he laughs.

"Anyway, as you might imagine, I've *always* had someone by my side. First, it was Winter or Summer, and when I got older, a boyfriend. It got to the point where I felt I *needed* to be in a relationship to feel okay, to feel whole. I guess it doesn't take a genius therapist to recognize the relationship pattern: trying to recreate the bond I have with my identical sister."

What is it about this man, who I don't even know, who I will speak to this one and only time, that's making me divulge some of my innermost thoughts? Via a computer screen no less.

"Anyway, I'm in my mid-twenties now and I'm determined to experience life unattached."

He smiles wide, revealing perfectly aligned teeth. "I admire that."

Heat spreads through my solar plexus.

"You moving?" he asks.

"Huh?" I respond, confused at the abrupt topic shift.

"That cardboard box there. Behind you."

I look over my right shoulder, noticing the big brown box I thought I'd moved far enough out of the way so it wouldn't appear on camera. I've lived in this apartment, this cozy one-bedroom in a mid-century modern building, for five years. Winter lives in a similar unit two floors below me.

I shake my head. "Not moving. That box has clothes I'm collecting for refugees from the Ukraine. One of those pet projects, something I do when I'm not working at the tourism board."

At that moment, Zippers the chihuahua wakes and puts his front paws on my shin, asking to be picked up. I do.

"And you have a dog?"

"Nope. Greta's fostering him while I find him a good home."

"So in addition to guitar, it seems like your hobby is...helping people."

"I'm a fortunate person. Not wealthy, like yo— but I have security, a loving family, good friends, the works. And as JFK once said, 'To whom much is given, much is required.'"

Ren's eyes dart downward to his desk. "Leah's texting me. Apparently, I'm due at a meeting in moments."

Well, that was a waste of 15 minutes, but a relatively painless one, at least.

"Listen," he continues in an expedient, confident tone that reveals why he's been so successful, "there are mutually advantageous reasons for both of us to accompany the other to two important events — your sister's wedding and my conference, which happens to be in your town. In other words, it sounds nuts but the fact is we both have motives for needing a faux date."

He's right. After all, what's the harm of two consenting adults benefiting from a fake relationship? Plus, I kind of like how a grown man used the word faux.

"A fair exchange...," I muse.

"Look, we don't have to decide just yet. How about if we meet in person? To ensure we're both comfortable with this idea. I just got a new car and was thinking about taking it for a long drive this weekend anyway. I'll head up to Lake Lyla and, if we continue to agree, we can hammer out the details of this arrangement."

"A long drive? I'm more than 300 miles from you!"

"I need to head up there anyway sometime before my conference. Need to visualize the location where I'll be giving speeches, moderating panel discussions."

I recall my days on the college debate team. Whenever we traveled to another university for a competition, I'd arrive at the classroom space early to check out where we'd be presenting our hard-fought arguments. It helped with my mental preparation. So I nod. "I get it."

"How about if I have my assistant Leah contact your" — his smile twinkles — "assistant Greta to set up the place and time?"

I look over at my friend, who's shaking two thumbs up at me. She's wearing the familiar, let's-get-into-some-trouble expression I remember from high school.

"Okay," I exhale, certain I'm needlessly agreeing to the most cockamamie plan ever. "I normally don't do stuff like this, but...it's a deal."

Chapter 7

REN

Looking back, I was so enamored with the solar system as a kid because I saw my own life mirrored in the planets, in the constellations.

In my small family, we circled *around* each other but weren't intertwined. I knew my parents loved me. In fact, they told me often that they worked as hard as they did to give me — and my grandmother — a good life. We both deserved it, they said.

And I did have a good life in the objective sense. We lived an upscale ranch-style house in a safe, suburban neighborhood. I was sent to the best private schools. I had the love and care of my grandmother instead of a string of babysitters to take care of me.

There's some debate among astronomers and others who study the cosmos about whether the solar system is an eco system or an exo system. Are the planets a community of living organisms working together? Or are the planets merely existing in an environment together, affected by one another but not working in conjunction? I'm not sure of the answer myself, though I am funding the research of a UC Berkeley scientist who's working to find out.

What I *do* know is that my family was more like an exo system. We love each other but we are not, have never been, intertwined. Growing up like that impacted the way I've moved throughout the world at large. I'm close to very few people: Leah, my grandmother, two people, incidentally, who happen to also be disinterested in my wealth. As a surprise for my grandmother's 70th birthday, I bought her a new house. While she appreciated the gesture, she declined the deed and the key, which I'd tied with a red ribbon, preferring instead to stay in the condo she's lived in since I graduated from high school. I was disappointed, but I sold the house and put the proceeds in a special account in her name that I'll tell her about someday.

Magazine profiles have portrayed me as a lonely, billionaire bachelor. (One recent headline read, "Cute, Companionless Castillo.") But I'm not lonely — I have people I care about deeply, I do cutting-edge work I'm obsessed with, I have personal interests that I have the means to explore with abandon. This image of me as the business world's most lonesome rich guy fuels the "let me set you up with my daughter/niece/friend/sister" frenzy that has become annoying in addition to just distracting. I've considered commissioning a magazine profile showing all the ways I'm happy as a bachelor, happy on my own.

But I'm certain that'll be met with a chorus of "the billionaire doth protests too much."

The synagogue is part cabin, part holy refuge — small and un-expectedly beautiful. The crowd is exuberant as synagogues around the world surely are on this day, Rosh Hashanah, the beginning of the Jewish New Year. I'm in Lake Lyla, the small mountain town at the northeast corner of California, about an hour south of Oregon and west of Nevada, and the location of the Infinity Symposium in a few weeks. Tomorrow I'm meeting Autumn Sky, the woman who, assuming we officially agree, will take me as her pretend new boyfriend to her sister's wedding and then accompany me to the conference here after that.

When reading about Lake Lyla, on the website of the very tourism board where Autumn works, I was surprised to learn there's a decent-sized Jewish community up here. And seeing as today is the Jewish New Year, I drove up a day early to attend services here instead of at home in San Francisco.

I'm greeted at the grand wooden door by an older gen-tleman holding a basket of yarmulkes, the traditional head covering. He lifts the basket with a smile, which I return, and then pull my own yarmulke from my pocket. I've been using the same one for more than a decade – my grandmother crocheted it in blue and gold, my college's colors. I place it atop my head and grab a prayer book from the table in the foyer and head inside the sanctuary.

I take a seat toward the back on a pine bench, with attrac-tive knots and the occasional dark stripe on the crisp blond wood. Tall and skinny, the windows highlight the magnificent scenery outside – mountains on the left, a canyon on the right. Trees of all kinds surround in every direction, casting warm, shifting shadows inside.

I considered taking my plane home for the holiday. But, as usual, my parents are both busy working and this year my grandmother decided to travel to her sister's to celebrate. I miss my grandmother on days like this. We had fun together on holidays when I was a kid. After attending services with my religious school friends, my grandmother and I would sneak extra honey chews from the basket afterwards and race each other to find the hidden matzoh after long Passover dinners even though it was a tradition meant solely for kids.

I don't go to synagogue much anymore. But now that I'm here in this surprisingly homey, peaceful place, I'm glad I came. The rabbi, who I'd seen schmoozing out in the foyer, now walks up the center aisle. He grabs a guitar that's resting on a bench and begins to strum Tichlech Shana, "May a Year of Blessing Begin," one of my favorite tunes. Within two notes, the congregation begins to sing along and I join in as well. Though I've never been to this particular synagogue before, it's all familiar. My whole life, I've marveled that Jewish people all over the world, from Morocco to Kansas, observe the same rituals during weekly Shabbat services and on ancient holidays. There's something poignant and humbling about it, and it makes me feel connected to my ancestors, most of whom I never met, as well as strangers I never will.

When that song ends, the official service begins. The rabbi is ebullient and charismatic, drawing with his words both laughter and nods from the congregants. We sing more songs and recite prayers offering gratitude for being alive another year. And his sermon is a terrific speech about inclusion, equality and justice, drawing unexpected analogies to a recently released Marvel superhero movie. As the formal service winds down, and he strums Oseh Shalom, "Praying for Peace," on his guitar, I take a moment to gaze around the room.

Elderly people wave and whisper to each other. Young parents shush stir-crazy toddlers. When I glance behind me to the right, I notice a familiar looking woman, which makes no sense because I've never been to this temple let alone this town before. She's studying the rabbi's guitar-playing, laser focused on his left fingers moving up and down the frets. I realize then that the woman is Autumn, the very person I am to meet tomorrow. Then I whip my head back around, remembering that she's got an identical sister.

Maybe the woman is Winter. But how to know?

Awkward.

The service ends and elementary school-aged children get the long awaited go-ahead to toss candy – honey chews, just like the kind my grandmother and I used to hoard – to the congregation to symbolize a sweet new year. The kids squeal and the grown-ups laugh, and it's hard to determine who is more delighted.

The rabbi strolls with his guitar back down the center aisle and invites everyone to follow him out of the sanctuary and into the foyer for the traditional blessings over wine and bread. There's a cheerful commotion as everyone gets up from their seats and gathers in the entryway, which within moments grows muggy from so many people packing into the small space. Some fan themselves with the synagogue newsletter that was tucked into the prayer books.

We gather around the rabbi, who stands before at a small table with a traditional round challah and a fancy cup for the ceremonial wine. When I look left, I discover I'm standing right next to Autumn/Winter.

Holy shit. Then I laugh inwardly given that I'm in a house of worship.

I wish Leah was here to advise me about what to do or to at least break the ice by confidently addressing the woman herself. But before I can decide what, if anything, to say, the woman widens her eyes at me. "Excuse me, are you...Ren?"

"So it *is* Autumn. I thought I recognized you but I wasn't sure if it was you—"

"—or Winter." She finishes my sentence. "Believe me, we're used to it. I've had people I've never laid eyes on before gather me into a tight hug meant for my sister. But what are *you* doing here?"

"Um, celebrating Rosh Hashanah? Just like you."

A teenage girl approaches with a platter of one-inch cups of wine. I take one.

Autumn shakes her head and asks, "Grape juice?"

The girl juts her chin to the left. "My brother's coming around with the juice tray right behind me."

When he does, Autumn takes a tiny cup of juice and then looks at me. "I mean, what are you doing *here*, at High Holiday services in Lake Lyla. I mean, I didn't think.... You showed me the map. Of Argentina. Your ancestors. Wait — did they escape Eastern Europe by way of South America?"

"Logical guess, but no." Normally, I'd play up the incongruity of my last name and my Jewish heritage, but since Autumn curtailed awkwardness by saying hello first, I decide to set her straight right away. "I know, no one expects someone named Ren Castillo to be Jewish."

She nods, looking relieved that I stated outright what she'd been thinking.

"One set of my grandparents was from Argentina, like I mentioned on our call. But my mother's family were Lithuanian Jews. My grandmother, who lived with us and was my primary caregiver growing up, is quite observant."

"Same! My dad grew up Episcopalian. My mom is Jewish. We were raised Jewish."

The congregation begins singing the prayer over the wine. I lean down and whisper, "Is your family here?"

She shakes her head. "My parents are in suburban Philadelphia for a housesitting gig so they're attending services there. My brother's in college in Chicago. Among my sisters, I'm the only one who's observant."

I'm relieved because I'm definitely not yet ready to begin the charade of being this woman's pretend boyfriend, if that's what she agrees to after we discuss it more.

"Interesting," I say. "Why you and not your sisters?"

She gulps the tablespoons of juice. "Jewish summer camp. One of the very few things I did without my sisters. Well, actually, the first year we all went together. But I was the only one who liked it so I returned for many summers after by myself. In addition to all the normal camp stuff — horseback riding, arts and crafts — I loved singing and dancing on Shabbat, baking challah, making our own Shabbat candles, hearing sermons about the values of kindness and responsibility, and just all the rituals."

"I get that. I went to Jewish camp too. Laurelwild, in Southern California."

"No way! One of my friends from college went there."

"Who?"

"Jake Miller."

"I remember him! He broke his leg on —"

"—the ropes course! He told me."

We shake our heads at the serendipity – of us meeting here, a day ahead of our scheduled meeting, of learning we both loved Jewish summer camp, of even knowing someone in common.

"Camp was dope," I say. "Sleeping under the stars on backpacking trips, ridiculous talent show skits...."

"My mom says I got my 'bleeding heart' from camp. I always opted for the do-gooder activities, like planting new trees or writing letters to elders, instead of climbing trees or learning archery. The whole notion of tikun olam, 'repairing the world' through personal action, to doing what I could to alleviate suffering...I just connected to that idea then."

"Autie!" A tall, self-assured man slings his arm around Autumn. "Happy new year."

"Oh hey, Noah. Same to you." She pushes her glasses higher on her nose, then holds a palm to the sky, gesturing towards me. "This is my, um...this is Ren. Ren, this is my colleague Noah."

Noah takes a beat before extending his hand. "Hey, man, how you doing?" We shake.

He edges closer to Autumn so the side of her head brushes up against his shoulder. "Heading into the office later?"

"Nope. Decided to take the whole day off for the holiday."

He nods his head vigorously, more than necessary, then rests his eyes on me again. I float the crown of my head skyward the way I used to do as a kid when my grandmother measured my height with a ruler, wall and pencil.

"Well, then, I guess I'll see you tomorrow in the office?" he says.

"You will."

He nods at me and makes his way back into the crowd.

Autumn and I stare at each other. She's even prettier than she appeared in her profile photo and when we video chatted. She wears eye glasses that highlight her cheekbones. Her skin is creamy, with the remnants of a summer tan, and her green dress features sexy curves. I feel my lower half stir.

She looks away and, like others in the room, fans her face with the synagogue newsletter. "Jeez, it's hot in here."

"Of course it is. As we Jews know, no matter when the High Holidays fall on any given year and no matter what the weather the day before or the day after, it's –"

"—always hot on Rosh Hashanah," we conclude simultane-ously.

She stills the makeshift fan and then narrows her eyes. "Ren, why are you here *now*? I thought you were just driving up for the day tomorrow. For our meeting to discuss, you know...."

I step to the side and place my empty plastic cup on the tray with other discards. "Planned to. But I was reading up about your town — on a particularly well-written tourism website, I might add — and learned about this 'cabin-like synagogue with a relaxed vibe where everyone is welcome.' Figured it was as good a place as any to celebrate the start of a new year."

"I wrote that website copy."

Of course she did.

Worshippers begin filing out of the building and into the parking lot, getting into cars to resume their day, Rosh Hashanah being a more low-key and festive holiday, as op-posed to its somber companion, Yom Kippur, the Day of Atonement, which is a couple of weeks away.

"So," Autumn says, moving hair behind her ear with her index finger. She has tiny, delicate hands. "Since we're both here, should we just have our meeting today instead of to-morrow? Maybe even...now?"

I remove the yarmulke from my head and do my best to tame the resulting static from my hair as we follow others out the door. "No time," I cringe at the cheesy response even as it's leaving my mouth, "like the present."

Chapter 8

AUTUMN

I didn't think I was using anybody, but looking back, I'm not so sure.

It started with Max, who I asked out in high school when it was clear that Winter's relationship with her first boyfriend Luke was not merely a passing thing. I was not getting my sister — my kindred soul — back to myself any time soon. So when I heard through the senior class grapevine that Max liked me, I got proactive and asked if he wanted to go see the latest James Bond movie. Without thinking too much about it, Max and I were soon a thing the way Winter and Luke were a thing.

And I liked Max. I did. But I see now that he was just the first in a series of placeholder relationships — boyfriends who were available, who kept me company, who could serve in the role of partner, sexual and otherwise. To be sure, I was in love with many of these boyfriends. Nick, the sensitive and extremely hot baseball player in college. Jaden, the personal trainer I dated in my early 20's. But that I liked them was often a problem. Because when a man could slide right into the longtime role that Winter had left *and* I really liked him? That was a recipe for neediness. Disaster.

It was as much of a disaster when it was the other way around — when the man really liked me and I saw him more as just "the boyfriend for now." (Because I always had to have a boyfriend. Always.) Then I'd find *him* needy whenever he wanted more of me than what I wanted to give.

A visual: I have sobbed at a man's feet, my arms clasped around his calves, begging to stay together. And men have sobbed at mine for the same reason.

I couldn't seem to get it right.

And it wasn't until Will, my last boyfriend, that I finally saw the unhealthy pattern for what it was. I liked Will a lot. He was one of the men I wanted more of, not the other way around. When old habits emerged — me calling too much, me just assuming, expecting that every free weekend hour would be spent together — Will tried to establish healthy boundaries. But I wouldn't adhere, feeling rejected instead by what I see now were reasonable requests.

When he broke up with me just a few months ago, I finally heard what I'd long ignored.

"Not everything needs to be shared, Aut," Will said. Tall with jacked muscles, Will fit my standard boyfriend criteria. But he was also a psychologist who laid out our problems in precise terms. "Relationships aren't about being the center of someone's universe or making them the center of yours. Aut, I don't think you even know what you're really, truly looking for because you don't know who *you* are."

It was the first time a breakup didn't absolutely shatter me because what he said actually made sense. It finally clicked for me: I had to spend time with myself.

Moments after he walked out the door, I pulled out a notebook and began writing a new diary, a practice I'd given up after high school. The first entry: "I pledge that before diving into yet another relationship, I will spend time alone, be single. Before I can truly commit to lifelong love, I commit to Autumn. *What am I all about?*"

Coffees ordered, Ren and I grab a table in the corner near the fireplace at Bernie's. I pull from my canvas bag a pad of paper and a pen. Ren pulls out a stylus and fires up an iPad. It's understood that we're not writing a *literal* contract — I'm sure Ren's cadre of lawyers could do that for us — but memorializing a personal, informal agreement. Nat King Cole's Unforgettable plays softly from the speakers mounted to the ceiling above our heads.

"Okay," I say, adopting a professional tone in the hopes that I sound far more confident than I actually am. "Down to business."

"Let's do it."

"First," I say, jotting my words as I speak them, "Under the auspices of being a new boyfriend, you will accompany me to my sister Summer's wedding."

"Correct. Related events?"

"Thanks for the reminder. Yes, the reception after." I underline the words "wedding" and "reception" in my notebook.

When he's not writing, Ren twirls the stylus around his fingers like a studious circus performer. "When not fulfilling 'boyfriend' duties, I'll be at the Inn, preparing for my conference."

"Which brings us to part two of this arrangement. I will then accompany you to any events during that multi-day conference where a companion is required and-or beneficial to you."

"I'll ask Leah to comb through the schedule. It'll include things like post-seminar cocktails, a gala one evening, et cetera."

"And after each event, I will return to my own apartment."

He points the stylus at me. "This contract must explicitly note that we're *both* getting something out of this arrangement. You get family and friends off of your back about dating because they'll believe I'm your new boyfriend."

"Exactly." It's unclear whether anyone will fall for it, but I'm willing to give it a try. I point my pen at him. "And *you* get the benefit of having a companion at a conference at which you would otherwise be bombarded with offers for dates. Fortunate hunters and such."

He laughs. "That's one way to put it. So, to confirm: we are each *aware* of the benefits the other is receiving by this arrangement."

"Yes."

"And we're both *agreeing* to it."

Consent is sexy. "Yes."

"And we're *both* getting something we need from this plan."

"Indeed."

"And once the arrangement ends, we...." He coughs. "Part ways."

I slap my palms together as if I'm a baker shaking off excess flour. "Done and dusted."

He leans back in his chair. "In my business, parties typically have a post-signing meeting after a big deal closes. A project retrospective. Just to hammer out lessons learned, evaluate the success, et cetera."

"That sounds wise," I agree. "Let's officially conclude our arrangement by meeting again after your conference. Here at Bernie's?"

"Duly noted," he says.

"But after that, no post-contract stalking!" I add, scribbling in my notebook. "In fact, no contact afterwards whatsoever. Seriously, write that down. Even if we become friends or whatever, this must remain a limited time thing. After all, we each have goals to pursue beyond these events that we both just need to...get through."

He holds up his iPad. "Purely a business relationship prompted by our assistants."

"The brainchild of Greta and Leah," I confirm.

Which, I hate to admit, was a smart idea.

"We should add," I continue, "that there will be Zero. Money. Exchanged." In my notebook, I surround the three words with three sweeping circles.

He lowers the corners of his mouth and nods admiringly.

"Well, for God's sake, Ren, don't look at me like that. I'm not a prostitute."

"Of course you're not. And neither am I, by the way. I guess I'm just used to people figuring out how they *can* get money from me."

I put my pen down and regard him. "That must be tiring."

He, too, stops writing, but continues flinging the stylus around his fingers. "I'm used to it," he says without a trace of self-pity. "That's one of the many reasons Leah is so valuable to me. She's an excellent judge of character. And plays bad cop whenever necessary."

"Well, I assure you, there will be no need for a bad cop in this case. I am fully aware that this is a stop-gap arrangement where the sole compensation for my role is you masquerading as my date for discrete wedding-related events."

Bernadette approaches our table. "One pumpkin spice latte."

I raise my hand. "Me."

Ren wrinkles his nose in what appears to be disapproval.

"One maple latte."

"Here," he says. "Smells good."

"Finally perfected the recipe this week. Let me know how you like it," Bernadette says before returning to the counter.

An old James Taylor classic plays from the speakers and I make a mental note to add the song to my try-to-learn list for guitar.

"This agreement," I say, "should it have a name? You know, something the two of us can refer to without risk of revealing the *true* nature of our relationship to anyone else."

"Solid idea."

"How about...?" I take a sip of my latte as I think. The cardamom and ginger is accented with a hint of lemon peel. The scent and taste is nostalgic, reminding me of baking with my mom after school on blustery fall days. As I bat different name ideas around in my brain — "Operation Faux Fling"? — I wonder if all of this energy is even worth it.

A friend of Winter's spots me from across the cafe. She waves and I wave back.

"You know a lot of people around here," Ren says.

"I've lived in Lake Lyla my whole life, minus four years of college. Come to think of it, for this whole thing to be believable, people already starting to see us together is probably helpful."

And then the name for our plan occurs to me.

"Have you ever seen Pretty Woman?" I ask.

His cheeks pinken. "Once or twice."

"So as you know, Edward and Vivian make a deal — she accompanies him to various events while he's engaging in a corporate takeover. Although she's a hooker, she's also a skilled professional, enabling Edward to have a companion without 'romantic hassles.'"

"Like I said, I've seen it."

I sit up straight. "Right. Sorry. So after getting her all gussied up, he says he's going to take her to an elegant restaurant called—"

"—The Voltaire."

Impressive.

"So how about we call what we're doing 'Operation Voltaire'?"

"Works for me."

We each write down the name.

"And another thing," I say, "we're going to need a backstory."

"Like a 'Meet Cute!'" He says the words like he's just provided a winning answer on a game show.

I stare at Ren, the powerful but nerdy, almost boyish, billionaire. His whole vibe is...incongruous, maybe even a little mysterious. "Precisely. We've got to get it straight now. Saying we met 'online' is too cliché, not really believable, especially because I've announced to several friends and my sisters that I don't want to be dating. So I wouldn't actively be on a dating site."

"How about if we say we met at synagogue?"

Genius. "We kind of did, didn't we?"

"Not only is it believable," he says, "it'll be easy for us to remember because it's mostly true: I came to Lake Lyla early to scope out the Inn and we started chatting in the foyer after new year services—"

"—we discovered we'd both loved Jewish camp, yada yada yada. Let's take a selfie together when we're done here today so we each have 'proof' on our phones."

The door to Bernie's opens and a gust of wind tunnels inside.

"Ooof," Ren says, wrapping his hands around his mug. I notice for the first time that his hands are large, his forearms muscled. "Sure cooled down since services this morning."

"That's fall in Lake Lyla for you. So, in addition to the Meet Cute, we need other details to make this plausible. My sisters, especially Winter, will see through flimsy BS."

"Details such as?"

"Nicknames?"

"'Ren' is already a nickname. Full name is Warren."

"Good to know," I say, jotting it down. "Maybe I call you Warren when I'm playfully mad or something. You can call me Aut or Autie."

"Not 'honey' or 'darling'?"

I'm thankful his tone is playful. "Hard no," I confirm. "I've always hated when friends use those syrupy terms with boyfriends. Gives me the willies."

"Same," he says, tipping his head back to finish the last drops of his latte. His Adam's apple is large, his chin covered in the beginnings of a five o'clock shadow even though it's mid-day. I happen to love facial hair.

That reminds me...

"One more thing," I say. "We need a physical intimacy clause."

Ren nearly chokes on his espresso. "A...what?"

"If we're to be a truly credible couple, we're going to need to hold hands, maybe give pecks on the cheek. Perhaps even the lips. We have to engage in some PDA – mild, of course – to prove our connection."

Ren licks milk foam from his lip. "Good point."

"One last thing—"

"Wait, have you ever done this before?"

"What do you mean?"

"*I'm* the billionaire business guy but *you* seem to be thinking of everything."

Involuntarily, heat travels to my ears and to my toes from the compliment. "Just want to be sure we're covering all bases. I especially don't want to be accused of taking advantage of your...situation."

"So what's the last thing?"

"When you're with me for phase one, the wedding stuff, I don't want it to be obvious that you have...money."

He draws his eyebrows together.

"Look at you," I say, pointing with my pen to his sweater, his jeans, his shoes. "Let me guess. Armani? Ralph Lauren? Canali?"

He glances down at this outfit. "Bally," he whispers.

Yuck. But at least he doesn't wear fake casual clothes like hoodies and $500 jeans like some of the tech bros who pass through Lake Lyla.

I slurp the last sips of my latte and toss my notebook into my bag. "Grab your things. I'm taking you shopping."

Chapter 9

REN

We exit the coffee shop and Autumn takes a left down Chestnut Street, the main commercial street in Lake Lyla, according to the map I studied before driving up here. We have a Chestnut Street in San Francisco too. But this quaint Chestnut Street is Lake Lyla's main drag, a far cry from, say, Market Street in San Francisco, with its huge hotels like The Four Seasons or big department stores. Rather, this main drag is comprised of a string of one-story small businesses, like Bernie's, the homey cafe we just left. Next door, there's Dubin's, a combination kayak and ski shop, and an art gallery featuring local painters, sculptors and photographers. An ice cream shop called Swirls and other small shops dot the street.

"All boutiques?" I ask.

"By city ordinance," Autumn says, exchanging the glasses on her face for sleek aviator sunglasses she pulls from her bag. As soon as she puts them on, she doesn't just look pretty, she looks glamorous. "No chains or franchises allowed – keeps the small-town feel. We've got everything anyone could need. Movie theater, post office, restaurants – both fancy and dive-y – gourmet markets, bookstores, everything."

We continue south, and I hear the warm tones of "As Time Goes By" on a saxophone. We cross the street and I see the music is coming from a busker on the corner. When we get closer, Autumn reaches into her bag, pulls out her wallet, then drops a five dollar bill in the jar nestled in the musician's open sax case. After she's given him the cash, we stop to listen. A crisp breeze hits my skin like a refreshing splash of cold water to the face. A hummingbird flits past so fast I almost miss it.

The saxophonist finishes his tune and thanks Autumn for the donation. We continue walking another block in silence until Autumn stops in front of a store called Pampered Paws, with artfully arranged stuffed animals in the window and glittery collars hanging down with clear fishing line, making them look like large, colorful raindrops. She pulls open the front door.

"We're going *here* for new clothes? Should I be insulted?"

"Don't be silly, *hon*. I'm going to quickly pick up some treats for Zippers."

"Zip—?"

"Zippers is the little chihuahua Greta is fostering, the one you saw on our video call. It'll just take a sec. I mean, got anywhere else more important to be?" she asks over her shoulder, a flicker of mischief in her eye.

These things cross my mind: an acquisition contract for the purchase of Planetary Motors I need to review, sales reports from a rocket fuel company I'm interested in buying, not to mention the Infinity Symposium keynote address I need to prepare for. I only have the barest outline for that 45-minute talk about where I see space entrepreneurship headed in the next five years. I also need to read up on the panelists for a 90-minute discussion I'm moderating about atmospheric advertising.

"No, *babe*," I retort. "Nowhere to be."

She bypasses the treats section and heads right to a tiny clothing rack, grabbing a flannel dog jacket for cold days and a plaid collar and then heading to the register.

"No treats? Like forgetting the milk, the primary thing you need, on a grocery store run?" I ask.

With exaggerated movements, she grabs a bag of treats from a nearby display and plops it loudly on the counter. "This too, please." To me, she says, "Didn't forget." Her wily smile suggests otherwise.

After paying, she walks past me on her way out the door, her nose pointed upward as if she's too busy to chit chat because otherwise she'd have to confess that she's not just providing for but *spoiling* the foster dog.

We turn left out of Pampered Paws and a few storefronts later come to a place called Barnard's. Inside, the store is warm and has a woody scent. A quick glance around reveals that this is an upscale — but not luxury — store for casual men's clothes. There are khakis and everyday button-downs on display. Autumn marches to the back towards a sign on the wall that says, "Sale!"

"Aren't we here for clothes for me to wear to your sister's wedding?"

"That's right." She moves hangers from left to right with efficiency, the metal-on-metal squeak making my ears itch.

"I assumed I'd wear one of my tuxes – or a suit at very least."

She stops moving the hangers and looks up at me. "*One* of your tuxes?"

I cough. "Isn't a wedding kind of a formal affair?"

She shrugs and resumes looking at the shirts on sale. "Maybe the ones you go to in San Francisco. Summer and Cole's will be casual, a lakeside ceremony with a small dinner in a restaurant private room after. What size do you wear?"

she says as she lifts a shirt off the rack and holds it up against my body. My scalp tingles from the gentle touch.

Before I can even reply "medium," she silently she shakes her head and replaces it on the rack.

"I *have* casual clothes," I insist, following her to a second sale rack.

"I know, but if you're to be my *boyfriend*," she says in a hushed tone, "then you've got to take it down a few notches." She appraises me from top to bottom. "No one will believe that *I* have gone ga-ga for a guy who wears five hundred dollar shirts. I work for a nonprofit. I organize charity drives and fundraisers. No one would believe I'd fall for a showy billionaire."

Showy?

I lean down and whisper back, "No one has to know."

Again, she stops scrolling through the rack. "They'll know if you wear that," she says, pointing to my Armani belt and Hugo Boss jacket. "Anyway, I have a hunch this'll be good for you. When was the last time you went budget shopping anyway?"

I don't answer because that would require confessing that I haven't looked at a price tag in years. Plus, she'd probably be horrified to know that I don't actually *go* shopping. Rather, Leah has clothes brought to my office every four months and I spend 45 minutes trying things on, making a neat pile for "keep," and then Leah takes it from there. So instead I quickly grab a random pair of pants from a nearby shelf and hold them up. "How about these?"

Autumn widens her eyes. "*Orange*? Orange *corduroy*?"

I look for the first time at what I'd grabbed.

"Yeah, probably not a good look for a lakeside wedding."

We continue roaming around, Autumn grabbing shirts and pants, and eventually she leads the way to the dressing rooms.

"Try these on with these, and these on with these, and this sweater with all of them. And I'll go grab some shoes up front to go with them. What size do you wear?"

In the dressing room I put on nondescript khakis and a pink shirt and see in the mirror that in some small, subtle way, I look different. While I've never been a fancy person, saving my tuxedos and suits for when they're truly necessary, I have in recent years become accustomed to fine clothes. Here in this small town, boutique dressing room, I see myself in a way I haven't in a while: regular. In a way, I look more like myself than I have in a long time.

The slatted door to my dressing room shutters as someone knocks loudly.

"Yes?"

"You coming out or not?"

"You want me to model for you?"

"Of course I do, *hon*."

"You don't think I can decide myself if —"

"— Oh, come on out already. I just want to see how things are looking. Think of it like a reverse Pretty Woman shopping spree."

I step fully out of the dressing room and Autumn takes a few steps back so she can appraise the top-to-bottom view of the first combination. She puts three shoe boxes down and adjusts the shirt collar and runs her hands along the side of the pants, testing for fit.

Again, the tingles.

"By the way, while Pretty Woman is a magnificent piece of entertainment," she lowers her voice, "*our* arrangement does not involve the same power dynamic. Money doesn't make you any better than me or anyone else. And, for the record, I don't need fixing and neither do you." She steps back and re-evaluates my outfit. "What do you think?"

I glance down. "I like it."

I'm beginning to like you.

She's refreshing and surprising and generous and wise.

"Okay, let's get you a couple of more things – but not too much. This is, after all, a limited time arrangement."

Chapter 10

AUTUMN

Ren flips through the pile of folded clothes on the bench of the dressing room like a card dealer flips through a deck in Vegas. "Two khakis, one pair of no-name jeans, two polo shirts, a button down, a sweater and a pair of faux-leather loafers. Sure that's enough? Doesn't seem like much."

I put my hand on my hip. "This is probably more than my brother buys in a year. I think it'll suffice for our...purposes." I shoot him a knowing look. "I'll wait for you up front." I turn on my heel and walk toward the register, grateful for a few moments away from Ren, not because I don't like him but because I do.

In the last half hour, I've seen him change clothes several times and in each outfit he looks better and better. His legs are solid. He smells like rosewood. Thick chest hair creeps out from his neckline.

Billionaires are supposed to be gross — old men with wives four decades younger, money-grubbers who make their money off the backs of the less fortunate. Or pot-heads in hoodies. In contrast, Ren so far seems kind and thoughtful and endearingly enthusiastic about his work.

I'm not happy about this.

Had I known he'd be attractive and likable, I'd have stopped Greta's plan in its tracks. But now I'm stuck pretending this sexy billionaire is my boyfriend.

"All set," Ren says as he approaches the register counter with his stack of clothes. His hair flies in different directions from pulling so many shirts over his head and from the static electricity in the September air.

"Will that be all for you?" the man behind the counter says.

Ren looks at me like I'm the authority. "Yes," I confirm, my insides toasting from the glance. "That'll do it today."

The cashier rings him up and then hands a bag over the counter to Ren, who pumps it up and down. "Wow, pretty small shopping spree" at the exact same moment I think, *I can't believe how much he just spent.*

Outside, the wind blows my hair in front of my eyes, twisting it in the hinge of my glasses. I pull off my frames, untangle everything and sweep my hair into a low ponytail. I begin to huff onto my lenses to clean them.

"Allow me," Ren says, reaching for the frames.

He cleans them with the edge of his high-end shirt, which has a higher thread count than the fanciest sheets. He lifts them skyward and looks through them to check that they're no longer streaked.

"Uh oh," he says. "I need to get my vision checked because I see perfectly out of these."

I turn my mouth into a *yikes* shape. "Relax. No prescription on those lenses."

He hands them back to me and cocks his head. "Why's that?"

"I started wearing them this summer as part of a differen-tiate-from-Winter program. She doesn't wear glasses. Makes

82

me more of an individual to wear them, less likely to be mistaken for her."

"Whatever works," he says, hooking his fingers around the loop of this clothing bag and tossing it over his shoulder Santa-style. "Trying on clothes makes me hungry. Grab a quick lunch?"

My belly is all jumbled from this day — first Rosh Hashanah services, then unexpected time with Ren at Bernie's and then shopping. I don't even have to look at my phone to know that it's well into lunchtime and I could benefit from some protein. "Sure. Let's keep Operation Voltaire in motion."

"So, Ms. Tourism Board, what do you recommend?"

I bring my index finger to my chin and glance up. A yellow warbler flies southbound across the cloudy sky. The ficus tree in front of Barnard's sways in the breeze. "Do you like wraps?"

"*Rats?*"

"No, wraps."

"Wraps! Yes, love 'em."

"Then I know just the spot. It's on the next block."

We head left on our way to Chompers. The temperature outside has dropped ten degrees since the heat of services this morning. That's the thing about this time of year in Lake Lyla – part of the day can feel like peak summer, the lake filled with sailboats and jet skis, and the other part of the day the first inklings of winter become palpable, the sky growing overcast and misty. I suppose that's why I love September and October here – and not just because my name is Autumn. I love the *duality* of it. The in-between-ness, the out-with-the-old-and-in-with-the-new, the "September is the other January" feeling that the Jewish New Year and the fall give me.

On the corner a woman huddles against the side of a building. She's leaning next to a large canvas laundry cart filled to the brim and covered with a black plastic tarp held down precariously with bungee cords. She looks exhausted. There's a bench next to her but it has what's called "hostile architecture" — a slanted seat and metal armrests in the middle, both preventing her from lying down. Her arms are crossed in front of her chest and she rubs her upper arms with her palms.

I unwind the knit scarf from my neck and flatten it out. I approach the woman. "Okay?" I ask, lifting up the scarf. She offers me the faintest of nods and I drape it over her shoulders. She says nothing but uses her fingers to pull the edges of the scarf further up her neck.

As we retreat, I point to the end of the block. "The wraps place is right up there," I say to Ren, who's staring at me with an expression I can't quite decipher.

Inside Chompers, we order — a Caesar salad wrap for me and a chicken chipotle wrap for Ren.

"Hungry again already, huh?" the woman at the register says to me.

"Pardon?"

"Weren't you just here like, what, thirty minutes ago? Got a cajun wrap and an iced tea, if I recall correctly."

Ah...even hungry for wraps at the same time.

"Nope, not me. I have an identical sister. She must have been here earlier."

The woman looks me up and down, not buying it. The fake eyeglasses don't always make enough of an impression. "If you say so...."

We sit at a table near the door. As we're getting settled, I hear a knock on the shop window. I look up and there's Eve, a friend from high school waving wildly. I wave back. She looks as if she's about to move on, but then catches a glimpse of my companion and comes inside instead, her curiosity clearly piqued. She's always been like that. In high school, she wrote a column for the school newspaper all about the comings and goings of the social scene. Winter, Summer and I were each referenced in the column a few times, but never by name — rather, merely as "one of the Sky sisters."

"Hi, Autie," she says. I stand and give her a long hug, then introduce her to Ren.

"Nice to meet you," he says. "Would you like to join us?"

I widen my eyes. I'm not ready to officially hit the gas on our farce. I need to absorb our contract, the terms — including our imagined Meet Cute — devised mere hours ago. I need baby steps. Preparing my fake boyfriend's wardrobe was just about enough for today.

"Oh no," Eve says. "I'm actually on my way to meet someone."

Thank God.

"Just wanted to come in and see my old friend Autie."

I return to my chair, hoping Eve will take the cue to leave. But she doesn't.

"I hear Summer's wedding is almost here," she says.

"We're looking forward to it," Ren says, grabbing my hand.

What is he doing? I'm not ready yet.

Just then, our number is called from behind the counter and I pop up to go grab the baskets with our wraps. "Well, great to see you, Eve."

"You too. Nice to meet you, Ren. Can't wait to hear about the wedding."

Grabbing our order, I realize how hungry I am. As soon as I sit, I take a huge, indelicate bite of my wrap. "What were you thinking?" I say, my mouth full.

"Didn't you say this very morning that it would be good for us to start being seen together? Make this whole...thing...more believable?"

"Yes, but I guess *I* need time to emotionally prepare."

I wasn't trying to be funny but his response is a deep belly laugh that's contagious and makes me crack up too.

This whole situation is absurd.

"Well, that may be a difference between you and me. I just figure let's dive right in, get some practice in."

I take another large bite of my wrap.

He points his chin to the woman behind the counter. "I'm starting to see how tiresome it must be to constantly be confused for Winter."

"Tiresome is one way to describe it."

"How would *you* describe it?"

"Winter would say annoying AF."

He blinks. Then repeats, "But how would *you* describe it?"

I take a deep inhale. "Kind of soul-crushing, to be honest."

"Tell me more."

I take a sip of water and run my tongue over my teeth, hoping I don't have lettuce caught unattractively there. "Okay, some examples. Over the years, I've had people — teachers, for example — say things to me like, 'Are you you or the other one?'"

"Damn."

"Buckle up. There's more. Once Winter and I had the same summer job working at a local gym. On the first day, our boss said to us, 'Don't bother telling me who's who — I won't remember.'"

"Ouch."

"I've had friends phone me, furious, telling me they waved at me across a room the night before and I didn't wave back. I've had people ask why my hair was shorter yesterday. Look, I'm not going to pretend that I'm disadvantaged by it all. And there are far worse people to be confused with than Winter — she's terrific. Confident, determined. But it's definitely affected me in ways most non-identical people don't understand."

"I can imagine. I mean, my face — anyone's face — is mine alone. It's a primary part of what makes me *me*."

"There's a flip side, though, which is that having Winter near me gives me a sense of security, of contentedness, unlike any other person in the world. And that's the lucky part. But, even so, it's time I understood what it's like to be an individual."

"I get it. So how have you dealt with..." he waves his hands around "...all of it?"

"Well, Winter's way has always been to be more...Winter. It's one of the things I love about her. She's unabashedly herself, not matter what others say or expect. As for me...my instinct has been to cling tighter — to Winter, to our relationship, to romantic relationships. But I'm working on that."

"How?"

"Well, for one thing, I'm no longer going to attach myself to someone just because that's what I've always done. Hence the need for Operation Voltaire instead of a real date, to whom I might be tempted to attach myself. I'm going to take all that time and emotional energy I normally spend in a romantic relationship and instead figure out what I'm all about. "

"By...?"

"Remember I mentioned I tried — and failed at — pottery? That was after tennis lessons, a jewelry-making workshop and a poetry class." I shake my head at the embarrassing memory of reading my melodramatic ode to one of my many old boyfriends in front of the class. "So I picked up guitar. I did it not because I'm musically inclined but I was searching for something, trying to find my *own* hobbies, my *own* passions. Finding what *I* like has never come easy to me. Unlike you, for example, with your interest in maps, in space. Anyway, neither Winter or Summer plays an instrument so I thought I'd start there."

"And how's that going?"

"Pretty rotten."

He chuckles. "And you have all of your volunteer work, right?"

I nod.

"That's just yours, not Winter's."

"Correct. She helps me sometimes with events or getting the word out or whatever. But it's my thing, really."

"Do you have any, you know, favorite causes?"

"Not really. I'll pitch in for almost anything. Anything macro like climate change to the most micro, like finding one animal like Zippers a good home. I take a pretty broad view of tikun olam — I'll do most anything to repair the world. I draw the line at politics, though. My time is better spent elsewhere. I leave that to others."

"Me too," Ren says. "That's something I love about space. For now, at least, space transcends politics."

"Greta, my resident astrology guru, would agree with you."

"So is it ever just too hard?"

"What?"

"Being devoted to so many crusades, being so attuned to all the problems and injustice in the world, to everything that's wrong, everything that need fixing?"

I tilt my head. "No one's ever asked me that before."

Not even me.

He raises his brows and waits. He wants to understand me.

I work it out as I speak because I've never really considered this. "It brings me a sense of satisfaction, of peace to help others. You're right, it can be overwhelming...seeing just how much must be done, how much is wrong. And I do get down when efforts fail, like people still dying of cancer. But raising money, planning fundraisers, running drives, increasing awareness — it's what I *can* do. So even if I, alone, can't solve the problems, I can put energy towards change, towards healing and progress, and hope the effect ripples outward. Like, maybe the small number of people I do touch go on to help others. So maybe somehow my small efforts translate out into the wider world."

"Small steps, big strides."

"That's *exactly* what I mean."

I've never talked so in depth about this aspect of myself before, not even with Winter. In my family, my role as "do gooder" has long been accepted as fact rather than something to discuss, dissect or puzzle out. And while a past boyfriend or two might brag to his parents about my fondness for volunteer work, they wouldn't *ask* me about it. Maybe they'd ask what time they needed to meet me at a gala, but they didn't want to know about my *relationship* to the work the way that Ren is doing now.

We finish our wraps, and Ren scoops up used paper napkins and the plastic baskets. "Just going to dump these in recycling and compost and then head to the restroom."

"Sounds good," I say, grateful for the moment alone to process the unexpected turn in my day since services in the morning. But on second thought, as soon as he's out of sight, I pull out my phone to text Greta.

Bumped into Ren at synagogue then we went to Bernie's and discussed our arrangement then we went shopping for casual clothes for him to wear to Summer's wedding events. Just had wraps at Chompers.

Greta responds with exclamation points. What's it like to be fake-dating a billionaire?

When I think about how many hungry or sick people he could help with even a fraction of his fortune...

As I wait for Greta's reply, Ren exits the bathroom and walks past the cashier. Noticing the tip jar, he pauses, backs up and drops a crisp twenty into it before returning to our table.

Chapter 11

REN

After a week back at home, including a day-and-a-half business trip to Los Angeles for a meeting with a UCLA astrophysicist and a tour of a satellite start-up, I'm in my Prius heading back up to Lake Lyla for my "girlfriend's" sister's wedding.

I planned to have Matthew drive me in the van so I could get work done (along with my advisor Kenny, who'd accompany me) and leisurely peruse a new wine catalog I received from a grape-grower in France. But this morning I let Matthew and Kenny know that I decided to drive myself. I enjoyed my first rides alone to and from Lake Lyla when I was here before. I loved seeing trees turning gold while traveling through Butte and Shasta counties. Even though I knew I'd get behind on work and my prep for the Infinity Symposium, those solitary drives reminded me how much I like being by myself, being away from advisors, lawyers, funders, bankers. I am an only child, after all and, I've always thrived in solitude.

Driving myself also gives me the chance to crank up the stereo and listen to Garth Dietrich, an instrumental guitarist Autumn recommended during our last video call. Preparing for the official launch of Operation Voltaire, we quizzed each other about basic background details of each other's lives, those superficial facts a newly dating couple would certainly know. Middle names (Paige and Tomas), favorite colors (green and brown — "Brown?" she guffawed in disbelief), favorite foods (pizza and filet mignon), bucket list items (learning Spanish and visiting another planet).

The guitarist is someone Autumn's taken to listening to as she's teaching herself to play. He's got a mellow, surf-y vibe, much different from the classic rock and hip hop I'd normally be blasting in the car by myself. But I'm interested in this woman – despite my better judgment, since our relationship is purely transactional.

It's new to me, this wanting to dip my toe in someone else's world. For the last several years, ever since I hit the lists of the country's wealthiest entrepreneurs, the few women I've dated have wanted to become entrenched in mine, the world of private chefs and private jets and being limited only by one's imagination. This, I know, had nothing to do with me as a person but rather what I represent – security, glamour.

I take my time on the drive, stopping about an hour in for another Taco Bell meal. I stop again about an hour south of Lake Lyla to meet with a retired cartographer and fellow map collector I read about on a cartography blog. When I reached out to him earlier this week, he agreed to show me his collection of thematic maps of Southeast Asia and computer-generated maps of underwater terrain in the Pacific Ocean. As a thank you for a fascinating hour, I leave him with a Bordeaux from Chateau Marie.

Once in Lake Lyla, Autumn buzzes me into her building, a pale blue, five story mid-century modern building. When she answers the door to her individual apartment, I involuntarily suck in my breath. It's the fourth time I've seen Autumn, only the second time in real life. I've always found her attractive. But today she looks...radiant. Her hair, the color of ancient pine, is styled with gentle waves framing her face. Her skin is dewy, her eyes bright. She's barefoot and wearing sweats.

"Hey, *babe*," she says, welcoming me inside.

Her apartment is cozy and colorful, decorated with blankets, pillows, plants and nature prints, and peppered with tidy piles. There's a grocery bag labeled "Food Pantry" on the kitchen counter, which I can see from where I'm standing, that box of clothes for refugees now piled much higher than when I first saw it on screen a couple of weeks ago, and a stack of papers on her dining room table with "Spaghetti Feed Fundraiser" written in all caps on a sticky note. This woman doesn't not spend her free time shopping, painting her nails or reading celebrity gossip magazines. This is a substantive woman who walks the walk and talks the talk when it comes to helping others. It makes me tired just thinking about everything she does in addition to her full-time job at the tourism board.

"Thanks for coming." Her words shake me back to the moment.

"Of course," I say a bit stiffly. *This isn't good, these feelings of admiration, of attraction.* "I fulfill my end of all agreements."

"Just need to put on my dress. I'll go ahead and do that in the bedroom. You're welcome to change here in the bathroom." She points to a door in the hallway.

Hung in the bathroom are four small sepia prints of Lake Lyla from the early 20th century, according to labels in the lower corners. I change into the clothes we got at Barnard's and then examine myself in the mirror. In this outfit Autumn picked out for me, I look like the guys I went to high school with, the ones who were self-assured and way cooler than I was. I'm not sure if I like what I see. But I do like how I feel: calm and unrushed. I slip on my new loafers and exit the bathroom to find Autumn waiting outside the door.

She's wearing a flow-y pale green dress, bare-shouldered and understated. She's dressed up but not overly fancy. It's such a sharp contrast to the weddings of the daughters of business colleagues or even friends from college I've attended in recent years, all glitzy affairs that felt like they were designed for paparazzi, for social media posts rather than the spirit of the union.

At the exact same time that she says, "You look handsome" and I say, "You look beautiful." We laugh. The words are generic but I, at least, mean them. Her outfit, her demeanor — she's like...a fairy.

She lifts her shoulder-length hair up with her hands and spins around so her back faces me. "Do you mind?"

I bring my hands to the delicate zipper and unhurriedly raise it toward the nape of her neck. I feel my nerve endings light up with electricity. Her breath deepens, making me wonder if she feels it too.

"Thanks," she says her voice barely above a whisper.

Outside, in the parking lot of her apartment, I say, "Your car or mine?"

"Mine. You drove all the way up here already today."

"I don't mind."

"Also," she adds, "I know you enjoy wine, and I don't drink. So enjoy yourself and I'll be the designated driver."

We hop in her car, an old Honda with a manual gearshift. There's almost nothing sexier than a woman who drives a stick.

As we travel toward the lake, she reminds me who will be at the wedding. Her parents, Allison and Doug. Her sister Winter, who I will obviously recognize instantly. Winter's date Jack, an old friend of all three sisters back from their middle school days. Her sister Summer, the bride. Cole, the groom. Cole's mother who everyone calls Gammy, and his daughter Livvy. Autumn's brother Colin. Summer's neighbor and friend Theo and her very best friend Jules.

Ten minutes later, we pull into the parking lot of a private dock a bit east of Rowan Beach, the main public beach on Lake Lyla's north shore. A few yards into the lake sits the Eureka Queen, the large old-fashioned boat where Summer and Cole got engaged just over a month ago. At the end of the dock is a small chuppah, the Jewish marriage canopy, covered in yellow and red flowers and dark greenery. Red-chested robins bob up and down and around the chuppah.

I'm not sure what I was expecting but I'm struck by how remarkable this setting is. A deep blue, the water laps loudly in the afternoon breeze, creating a calming soundtrack suitable for an ASMR video. The mountains hover above, adding to the cozy, intimate feel. The fragrant mums, daisies and sunflowers (Autumn has identified the flowers for me) in the various bouquets make me almost lightheaded. Classical musicians serenade us with Haydn from the deck of the Eureka Queen.

When we reach the small group that's congregated at the end of the dock, Autumn introduces me around. Everyone is dressed as she predicted: no suits, no ties, no diamonds, no shimmery beads. Summer looks sweet and feminine in an off-white dress with a pale pink sash at the waist. Like Autumn and Winter, she's pretty, but I can tell immediately that she's different. Not only does she have a whole different look — lots of wavy hair, light blue eyes — but her manner, while friendly, is more self-contained. Cole the groom is decked out in navy, red and white in his full Marines dress uniform.

I'm met with convivial hugs from Autumn's sisters and mother and I'm struck by how different my upbringing was — with parents preoccupied with working, no siblings, my grandmother my primary companion. I wouldn't trade those times with my grandmother for anything. But it was lonely. I expected Autumn's parents to be like mine — polite but largely disinterested. My family is kind and affable, but nothing like the Sky family's effusive energy. They're going *in*. Her dad asks me all kinds of friendly questions about where I'm from, how I like Lake Lyla, how Autumn and I met. Her mom looks me in the eye, conveying genuine interest in my answers. Her brother uses my name every time he speaks to me. I see first-hand why Autumn needed some kind of decoy for this event. At this tiny, casual wedding ceremony, I feel a different kind of abundance than I'm used to — not money-based, but a familial, collective joy.

I also now see why people so easily confuse Autumn and Winter. The texture of their hair is the same (if not the exact color or length), as are their eyes, their cheekbones. Autumn would have to do a lot more than wear fake eyeglasses to truly differentiate her appearance. That said, I *feel* that the two of them are very different, if not in looks then in body language, in vibe. Whereas Autumn is sensitive and warm, I can tell after observing them together for just a few minutes that Winter is no-nonsense and bold.

As the group chats, I notice Autumn shivering. It's now late afternoon and fog is descending across the lake, adding to the beautiful, amidst-the-clouds landscape but also causing the temperature to dip.

Here goes.

I put an arm around Autumn, who leans into my embrace. Noticing the gesture, her mother grins at her husband.

Are we actually pulling this off?

Outside of Dungeons & Dragons games, I'm not used to role playing, to pretending in real life to be something I'm not. Luckily, there's no time for me to botch answers to potentially more probing questions because the officiant announces that it's time to begin the ceremony.

The group gathers in a tight circle. I feel at once as if I don't belong and also as if there's no other place I'm meant to be in this moment, even the most exclusive boardrooms or the most luxurious hotels I've become used to.

The ceremony lasts just a few minutes and is filled with laughter. Without even knowing the couple, it's clear that Summer and Cole are beyond happy together and his daughter Livvy is especially ecstatic about the marriage.

When it's over, Autumn slips her hand in mine, intertwining her fingers with my own. They're dainty and ice cold.

"Onto the party!" Cole says and everybody cheers.

I begin to follow the crowd off the dock but Autumn squeezes my hand and keeps me in place.

"Should we take a picture here?" she says in a confidential tone. "You know, more... evidence?"

I pull my phone from the pocket of my new khakis and extend my arm, hoping to capture not just our faces but the Eureka Queen on the lake and the fog, trees and mountains behind us. "A little closer," I say.

We mash our cheeks together so that we can both fit into the frame. I wonder if she can feel the heat rising on my face with the touch. I snap the picture and then review it, noting that she looks as sexy in it as she does in real life.

"Can you text it to me? I'm gonna post it," she says as we walk to the car.

"Good idea."

Once inside her Honda, we each upload the photo to social media. Autumn's caption says, "At my sister's wedding!"

I post mine — to my very, very private account — without a caption. Immediately, I receive my first like — from Leah. As we're driving to the reception, I get a few more likes from friends, a couple of map collector buddies and Matthew. I check again after a few minutes and see a private direct message from my longtime advisor Kenny. Suspicious, protective, risk-averse Kenny. In response to my post at the wedding, he's sent me two emojis: a pot of gold and a shovel followed by a question mark.

Chapter 12

AUTUMN

Driving from Summer's wedding on the lake to the Noble Peasant restaurant, Ren and I chat about the ceremony. He's distracted, though, focusing on comments and messages on the photo we each posted, another deliberate ploy to make Operation Voltaire believable. After all, these wedding events are only Phase One — there's still his multi-day conference to get through in a couple of weeks.

He tucks his phone into his pocket. "Cole seems like a good guy."

"He's the perfect match for Summer, exactly what she needed to help her recover from a relationship trauma from years ago."

"That Marines uniform...man, he's bad ass."

"Get a chance to chat with Winter?"

"Not yet. But she sure is pretty." I hear the wink in his voice.

"Compliment taken. Seriously, though, you'll like her. She can be bossy and intense, but fierce in her love for others."

We wind our way north, up into the wooded neighborhoods tucked into the side of one of Lake Lyla's many mountains. I'm amazed at how comfortable I feel with Ren, this man I hardly know. Maybe it's because this whole thing being pretend takes the pressure off, the pressure of making witty conversation, of digging around for things in common, of having to always present my best self, to not expose my clingy side. Maybe someday, once I've been on my own, I'll find this with a *real* boyfriend.

"Pretty dope," Ren says, pointing out the window to the neighborhood's large, organic boulders surrounding understated mansions. "I love San Francisco, love the bay and the bridges, Treasure Island, the distinctive neighborhoods like the Mission and Ashbury Heights, and Golden Gate Park and of course the ocean. But I see why your family settled here all those decades ago and why you all have stayed."

I downshift into second, then first and pull into the parking lot for the Noble Peasant. We park right next to Winter, her date Jack, my brother Colin, and Jules, Summer's friend, who drove with them.

Together, we enter the restaurant, decorated on the outside with white, twinkly lights and pots of sweet-smelling jasmine along the walkway. Once inside, I'm instantly enveloped in warmth, a notable contrast to the misty early evening outside. In just the last week, the days have grown noticeably shorter. Inside, the restaurant is lit with candles. Clay pots of white poinsettias hang from the ceiling.

The hostess guides us to the private room in back, a wood-paneled space that seats just fifteen. Summer is sitting at the large round table, flanked by Livvy and Cole. Her palpable joyfulness nearly stops me in my tracks. It's such a sharp contrast to even just a few months ago when she was still processing the anguish of years before.

Seeing us arrive, Summer gets up from the table, which is decorated with square, low-lying flower arrangements and photos. Summer and Cole hiking on Cloud Stretch, their favorite trail, with Livvy. Pictures of Cole growing up in Ohio, in his Marines fatigues, holding Livvy as a newborn. Pictures of Summer with me and Winter, with Jules, and with Livvy.

"Ren," she says, taking his hands into hers, "thank you for coming. I'm looking forward to getting to know you."

"Likewise," he says. "And mazel tov on your marriage."

"Picture, picture!" Jules says. I feel her hands on my shoulders, turning me so that my two sisters and I are facing her. We throw our arms around each other and smile for the camera like we've done a thousand times before.

Out of the corner of my eye, I notice an expression on Ren's face that looks like wistfulness, though I'm unsure if he's manufactured it simply for Operation Voltaire. I realize then that I got the better end of our deal. Maintaining this act in such an intimate environment must be stressful and exhausting. All I'll have to do is make small talk with random people at an impersonal business conference.

A waiter approaches with a tray of glasses filled with red and white wines. Everyone takes one but me. Ren brings his glass of red to his nose, swirls the liquid in a circle and then takes a sip.

I raise my eyebrows, as if to say, *And how is it?*

"Delicious," he says, puckering his lips slightly. "Rich and dark. High tannins but still balanced." He turns to the waiter. "Could I trouble you to bring out the bottle whenever you get a moment? I'd love to take a picture of the label."

Even though I'm squarely in the nonprofit world, I've witnessed my fair share of rich, entitled people, men and women, whether as tourists in my office or guests at the Inn or as potential donors to organizations I volunteer for. Most are aware of the effect their money has on others and even seem to take pleasure in that fact. It often comes out in how they treat people they consider to be beneath them or just in the way they move about the world, often with a distinct swagger or brashness. But I haven't observed that in Ren. Somehow Greta zeroed in on the rare unpretentious guy among all the possible matches on Billionaire Rendezvous. She informed me the other day that because I'm a Taurus, Venus is my ruling planet and, apparently even better, it's in my 12th house, whatever that means. Venus has been in retrograde, which has triggered my insistence in turning inward, which, she insists, will pass, and that Ren, a Virgo, is perfect in the meantime.

"Let me see your ring," Winter says to Summer, who holds up her hand. Her nails are polished in a pale pink and the simple platinum band is at once shiny and subtle, just like her engagement ring.

"Oh, Sum," I say, taking hold of her hand. "It's gorgeous."

Our parents arrive then, my dad joking that they're a few minutes behind everyone else because my mom had to collect herself in the car, so overjoyed she was by the ceremony.

With everyone now here, we sit down for dinner, a delicious fall feast complete with butternut squash soup, spinach and kale ravioli, and pear tart. Apple cider is served along with coffee to accompany dessert, and the spicy aromas make me almost dizzy with warmth.

Throughout the meal, Ren seems to be enjoying himself enough, laughing with Cole's mom, whose abrasive tone and no-nonsense words always crack people up. She has no shortage of funny stories about Cole as a kid. Then I overhear Ren telling her about growing up as an only child, just like Cole did. Their conversation is authentic and deep, which is amazing considering they met only a couple of hours ago.

On the other side of Gammy, Theo, Summer's avuncular friend and former neighbor, joins in their conversation, asking Ren what he does for a living.

"I work in space."

"An engineer?" Theo asks.

"An investor, an entrepreneur."

"Wait a minute," Winter's date Jack pipes up, pointing at Ren. "I *thought* you looked familiar. Couldn't place you at first. Is your full name Warren?"

"It is."

"I've read about you! In a recent issue of Executives magazine. You're like...the shit. You're not just 'an investor, an entrepreneur' — you're *the* investor, the country's leading space entrepreneur — the guy who sees possibilities where others don't. Wow, man, so cool."

Ren blinks and nods affably but modestly, his chin tucked. He looks down at his plate, at the crumbs of pear tart.

"You know," Jack says, "I have this super cool idea for an app. Everyone says it's a sure winner. Just need an angel investor to get the ball rolling...."

As Jack drones, Ren politely nods. It's stark how differently Ren is treated once his financial status is unveiled. It must be hard to be known for your money and not necessarily for yourself, to have to parse out peoples' true motives in getting to know you.

"Anyone seen the new Julia Roberts film?" I blurt. Ren tosses me a grateful look, evidently eager to step out of the spotlight.

After the dishes are cleared, speeches begin, starting with my dad choking up as he tells stories of Summer, the oldest, by minutes, of the three of us. Then Jules gives examples of what a supportive friend Summer has been. Livvy gets everyone's waterworks flowing as she describes how happy her dad has been since meeting Summer and how she's excited not just to have Summer as a step-mother but as a friend. Winter takes a turn next, saying, among other things, that Summer's relationship with Cole has renewed her faith in finding true love.

"So cheers to Cole and Winter — and to all the couples, old and new, here tonight."

Summer and Cole kiss passionately, the connection between them as sizzling as the embers burning in the corner fireplace. My parents bring their foreheads together and kiss tenderly just the way you'd expect of a middle-aged couple still very much in love. Winter plants her lips on the cheek of her old friend.

Suddenly, I feel all eyes on me and Ren. We look at each other, silently understanding what we must do. I struggle to keep alarm out of my expression. After all, this is something we expected. It's even part of our agreement, jotted down in the notebook that's out in my car out in the parking lot. Consent for mild PDA exactly like this has been predetermined. Ren leans toward me with both hesitation and resolve in his eyes, mirroring my feelings exactly. It's a silent acknowledgement that this is what we committed to with our unorthodox arrangement.

I bring the corners of my mouth up and lean forward. His upper lip lands above mine, soft and supple. He smells of merlot and expensive aftershave. There's a hummingbird in my chest, fluttering a dozen times in a single moment.

I barely register everyone's applause.

Chapter 13

REN

Even though I was never part of the popular crowd, I always had a small, core group of friends, usually fellow offbeat kids. And it was my grandmother who, through her example as well as her explicit wisdom, taught me how to relate to my peers. Affectionate teasing, inside jokes, spoken and unspoken compassion — I saw and heard it all when I lingered around my grandmother's weekly canasta and mah jongg games with her own longtime tribe.

I learned manners not through formal etiquette lessons but by watching my grandmother interact with grocers, delivery people, doctors. Anyone whose path she crossed was asked how *their* day was going before she ordered her decaf or signed for a package. To this day, she's still the last to hang up the phone, even after everyone has already said goodbye.

She instilled in me a love of crossword puzzles, the importance of stretching, the value of not giving a shit about what others think. She told me stories of my immigrant ancestors, demonstrated that age is just a number, brought me into silent hugs when she could tell I needed one. She made me feel special by inviting me along on errands, conveying that she simply liked my company no matter what we were doing, and by drawing funny faces with a Sharpie on the bananas that she packed in my lunches.

Perhaps most of all, though, she gave me insight into my parents. It was all too easy to be disappointed by their jam-packed schedules and by the priority they placed on work over family. It wasn't that they were never around — they were. But even when they were home, they were exhausted and often distracted.

Seeing this, my grandmother would address it with me head on. (Another life lesson: it's helpful to *talk* about it, whatever "it" may be.)

"They're hard-working, and that's an admirable quality," she'd say.

Or, "Talk to your friends with helicopter parents. That's *really* no fun."

But my favorite thing she'd say is, "Fuck it. We're awesome all on our own."

"Everything in order?" I ask.

"Transportation to the airport is lined up and the jet has been readied," Leah confirms with her signature efficiency.

We're having breakfast at The Aviary, one of the restaurants at the Inn where I've just spent the night after Autumn's sister's wedding. Leah and Samantha drove up yesterday evening so this morning we could survey the space where the Infinity Symposium will take place. The dining room is bright, with white walls and table cloths, and decorated with formal chairs covered in fabric with deep blue and green stripes. The centerpieces feature slim vases displaying rustic branches tied together with orange gingham ribbon. I've stayed at hundreds of five-star hotels, from Bangkok to Copenhagen to Martha's Vineyard. While not technically a five-star hotel, the Inn rivals any one of them. When I drove up yesterday, the magenta bougainvillea cascading down the crisp white front of the entrance was, to quote Leah, "utterly breathtaking." The service has been attentive yet blessedly low-key.

"Who *is* this woman?" Samantha asks, biting into a piece of buttered sourdough. One of my favorite things about Leah's wife is that she's supremely uninterested in our work, in my money. And she has a zero BS tolerance.

Leah's eyes meet mine and I infinitesimally shake my head. No one but the two of us — and Autumn and Greta — know the true nature of my "relationship" with Autumn, that it's contract-based, founded on mutual benefit rather than emotion. And I intend to keep it that way. It's not that I fear Samantha will tell anyone, let alone anyone at the conference where Autumn is to act as my girlfriend, but I want to keep it private because it feels disrespectful to Autumn to imply that I wouldn't be interested in her otherwise.

Because the fact is, I probably would be.

"Met her recently," I say, dismissively. "I'd like to do something nice for her."

Samantha's brows travel upward. "'Nice'? I'll say."

A waiter approaches and refills coffee into crisp white china from a shiny silver pot. I gulp a few large sips before wiping the corners of my mouth with a napkin and scooting my chair back. "Heading over now. If all goes well, I'll meet you in a little bit."

Leah gives me a thumbs up and sets a timer on her phone.

Fifteen minutes later I'm outside Autumn's apartment building, debating. Is it too early on a Sunday morning –

particularly the morning after her sister's wedding – to ring her doorbell when she's not expecting me?

To be on the safe side, I text.

Outside your building. Have something to ask you. If you're awake/home, can you come down or buzz me in?

Thirty seconds pass and it feels as if lead has formed in my abdominal cavity. I hadn't realized how much I was hoping to see her today, even though my obligation to phase one of Operation Voltaire is officially complete. I turn to walk back to my car, ready to tell Leah to call it all off, when I hear the harsh, mechanical tone of the front door unlocking. I turn and leap several feet to catch it just in time. When I reach her floor, I see down the hallway that she's leaning part-way out her apartment door, her expression confused, her hair tangled. She's wearing red and black plaid pajama bottoms and a t-shirt that's long lost its original shape.

As pretty and ethereal as she looked at yesterday's wedding, right now she looks...adorable.

Dude, I reprimand myself, *what the hell are you doing here?*

"What are you doing here?" she says.

I've walked too fast, too eagerly up the stairs and I'm a bit breathless. I feel just like I did in high school when I conned Leah into accompanying me to a frozen yogurt shop where a girl I liked worked and then asking for "banilla" with strawberries.

"Hi," I say willing my huffing to slow.

"Hi?"

"So, um, I know this isn't part of Operation Voltaire. But I figured since I'm here in Lake Lyla, it couldn't hurt to spend a little more time together. To make our connection seem real. You know, for the conference?"

She leans against the door jamb and places her hands in the pockets of her pajama bottoms. "I think it's believable already.

Winter just texted this morning wondering when *my* wedding will be." She shakes her head, then, as an aside, adds. "She's so aggressive sometimes."

I recall my lips touching hers barely twelve hours ago. Though its public nature was admittedly cringey, it was a great first kiss. Gentle, electric, arousing.

I nod. "So, um, you free today?"

She removes her hands from her pockets and crosses her arms, body language belying her provocative grin. "What do you have in mind?"

I respond with an exaggerated shrug, conveying that it's a secret.

"I suppose I can move some things around in my busy schedule," she says, equally guarded and playful. "I need to get dressed. The attire?"

"Casual. Jeans, something like that."

She widens the door and I cross the threshold into her apartment.

"You're lucky I'm someone who likes spontaneity. My sister Summer would hate this idea." She walks towards her bedroom. "Be ready in a few minutes."

"While you're at it, throw a change of clothes and a toothbrush into a bag."

She stops mid-hallway. "Um, what *is* this, exactly?"

"You'll be back well in time for work tomorrow. Promise."

We pull up to a rural patch of land about fifteen miles south of Lake Lyla.

"Okay, this has some serious serial killer vibes," Autumn says from the passenger seat of my Prius, pushing her glasses higher on her nose.

"Trust me."

Leah drives up a few minutes behind us, here, as she always is, to ensure everything goes precisely as arranged.

We get out of the car and I introduce Autumn to Leah, the two having previously only met on video.

"Everything's on schedule," Leah says, then points an index finger up and tilts her ear to the sky. "Wait for it...."

Sure enough, within about 20 seconds, the whirr of a helicopter masks every other sound as it slowly descends onto the empty land before us.

Autumn's eyes widen starkly as she takes in our mode of transportation. Leah puts a comforting hand on Autumn's shoulder.

"I get it," Leah says, "This billionaire bullshit can be weird. But just go with it. I've known Ren since we were in sixth grade. I assure you, there's not a more trustworthy billionaire out there."

Autumn chuckles and her shoulders drop about two inches.

"For real, if I were straight, which I'm not," Leah say, pointing a thumb to her car, "because I'm in love with my wife Samantha, I'd go for this guy. You're safe with him. And you might as well have a little fun because that conference you're going to with him? It's going to be boring AF."

We climb into the helicopter and place headsets over our ears.

"Can you tell me now where we're going?" Autumn says, her voice tinny through the speaker system.

"To my plane."

"*Your* plane? Your...*plane?*"

I nod and point out the window because as we ascend, Lake Lyla comes into view surrounded by trees turning gold and orange. Amidst the comfortingly still mountain peaks, the lake is crystalline and jewel-like.

Moments later, when Lake Lyla is no longer visible due to our northward trajectory, Autumn turns from the window to me. "I'm going to be home *in time for work* tomorrow?"

"I promised."

She shakes her head and mutters something to herself. Though I hardly know her, it's clear she's starting to have fun.

Soon, we're descending onto a small private airport just over the border in southern Oregon, my Bombardier Express is there waiting for us. Once aboard the aircraft, Autumn's demeanor switches from confusion and surprise to one of awe. She says nothing as she runs her fingers along the polished wood of the seat rests, the copper satin finishes, the linen seats. Her reaction is a reminder that I've become inured to the trappings of success.

We sit facing each other, a small table between us. After we take off, the flight attendant delivers lattes, maple for me, pumpkin spice for Autumn.

"It's not Bernie's but hopefully it's close enough," I tell her.

She glances at her phone. "How is it just ten-thirty in the morning? I got up barely two hours ago, sure that this was just an ordinary Sunday." She puts the phone on the table face down. "Where are we going, Ren? I know we're not heading to San Francisco for the opera like in Pretty Woman because," she waves her hands over her lap, "jeans."

"Seattle."

"Why?"

"Like I said, I thought it'd be a good idea for us to spend more time together."

"You said that. But why Seattle?"

"You don't like Seattle? Great music scene for a budding guitarist."

"I love Seattle. Everyone loves Seattle. But—"

"I wanted to take you somewhere fun, but also close enough that you'll be back at work tomorrow."

We land right about lunchtime. Stepping onto the airport tarmac, we're greeted with Seattle's quintessential damp smell and drizzle. Autumn pulls a wool neck warmer from her bag and pulls it over her head. Its bunchy, beige folds highlight her creamy skin and dark gold eyes, otherwise shielded behind her glasses.

"Hungry?" I say.

"Starving."

I lead her to an old, non-descript structure just to the left of the little airport's administrative building. "Welcome," I say, "to one of my favorite places on Earth."

Chapter 14

AUTUMN

One step inside Propeller Kitchen and I'm pleasantly bombarded by the smell of coffee, orange juice and that inexplicably inviting aroma of cooking grease. The tables are metal, the seating is worn pleather booths.

"Helicopters, private planes....they're cool," I say, "but *this* is my kind of place."

"Best grilled cheese on the planet," Ren says with as much pride as if he were the chef.

A waiter wearing a black apron greets us after placing two thick ceramic plates at a nearby table. "Mr. Castillo, welcome back."

"Nice to see you, Hank. Remember, it's Ren."

The waiter points to a corner booth, where we sit. Hank returns moments later with a plastic pitcher of water. "The usual for you, Ren?"

"Yes, thanks."

"And for you, Miss?"

"I haven't even looked at the menu, but," I inhale, "based on the scents, I think I'd like one of everything."

Ren lets out a boisterous laugh that makes me feel like a world-class comic. It triggers a pleasant but unusual feeling in my chest. Winter has always been the funny one.

"That," Ren says, "can be arranged."

"Kidding, of course." To Hank, I say. "I'll have whatever he's having."

He nods and slips away.

"A twist on a classic movie line," Ren says, sipping water from an opaque plastic glass.

"When Harry Met Sally is my mom's favorite film. Seen it countless times. As I've mentioned, Pretty Woman is mine."

"Not particularly macho of me to admit, but they're two of my favorites as well."

"Did you idolize Edward Lewis? Is that how you ended up with the life you have now?" I gesture out the window to where his jet is parked.

"Idolize isn't exactly it, but I did relate to him in some ways. His single-mindedness, his being an only child."

I interlace my fingers together, place my hands on the table and lean forward. "What other movies do you like?"

"Casablanca...."

"A classic, one of the few that's aged well. What else?"

"The Fugitive."

"Solid," I say with a slow nod. "Whenever I come across it while channel surfing, I *have* to watch to the end even though I know what happens."

"Stand by Me," he adds.

"My dad loves that movie."

"Another huge favorite," Ren says, "a small film you may not have seen: Searching for Bobby Fischer."

I shake my head. "Never heard of it."

"A 'perfect' film, according to my grandmother. It's about a young boy, a chess phenom."

"You into chess?"

"I have no idea how to play chess. But, like my grandmother, I've always loved the film, its moral: that no matter what heights one achieves, one must still live by one's values, must still be a good person."

His brow creases and his lips slightly purse and I understand then why the film resonates. The private plane, the pandering. It must grow hard to sift through the chaff, to stay grounded in reality, to zero in on the genuine. "Anyway," he adds, "I think you'd like it."

"Sounds not unlike the moral — one of them, anyway — of Pretty Woman. I'll add it to my list."

The waiter arrives with two stacks of pancakes. I raise my eyebrows at Ren. "Thought you said it's the grilled cheese that you love here."

"That's next."

"*Next*? Nothing comes *after* pancakes."

"Trust me – just have a few bites. I don't get to this place often enough so when I *am* here I eat bits of all my favorite dishes." He douses the pancakes with boysenberry syrup.

I do the same and take a bite. He's right. They're fluffy and buttery with just-right crispy edges. "So what's with the private plane, anyway?"

"What do you mean?"

"I mean, you can catch any number of flights from the Bay Area to, say, Seattle. Probably close to twenty options a day."

He wrinkles his nose the way my brother does when he's told it's time to clean the gutters at our parents' house.

I put down my fork. "Are you implying that commercial flights are for 'the riffraff'?"

"No, no. But they are kind of...Petri dishes of germs."

"You're not wrong but—"

Just then Hank arrives with two tall, cylindrical glasses filled with what looks like orange juice and with the unmistakable bubbles of champagne. "Mimosas," he says, placing them on the table.

Ren take a glass and raises it, clearly relieved to be interrupted from the discussion about why he doesn't fly commercial. I lift mine as well. He takes a sip and I place mine untouched back on the table.

"Don't like champagne?" he asks.

I don't want to get into it all now, not today. So I smile and say, simply, "Something tells me I'll be needing all my wits about me today."

When the sandwiches arrive I confirm his assessment: it's truly the best grilled cheese I've ever had. The perfect golden color, thick cheddar, a satisfying crunch.

We make idle chitchat, turning from movies to TV shows, discovering that we both enjoy British crime dramas but only with closed captioning on. I learn more about his experience as an only child, how it shaped him into an introvert. It makes his comfort traveling through life without a partner understandable. It's something I admire and aspire to – at least for a time. I like how he laughs easily and doesn't just ask me about myself but really listens to how I respond, a rarity among men I've dated.

Before I boarded the helicopter earlier, Leah pulled me aside, whispering additional assurances that Ren is the best of men. "Kind of an enigma," she explained. "He still thinks he's the geek he was in high school. I mean, he *is* still kind of geeky. The maps and all.... But he has no idea how hot he is now." And the more time I spend with him, the more I see that he really is hot. His thick dark hair begs for fingers to softly comb through it, his forearms are muscular and hairy.

I take a swig of ice water, keeping bits of ice in my mouth so I stay centered, present.

When we finish eating, Ren places cash on the table, and I notice that he's left Hank what probably amounts to a 150 percent tip. Outside, there's now a car waiting for us on the tarmac, a gorgeous gunmetal grey Tesla with gullwing doors open to the sky.

"Yours?" I ask.

Ren shakes his head. "Rented."

I can't help it. I'm enjoying the ostentatiousness, something I normally abhor. I focus on the positive fact that this is an electric car with almost no carbon footprint and ignore the fact that the vehicle costs far more than my annual salary and could feed a family in a developing country for a year.

I haven't been to Seattle in a couple of years so I gaze out the window as Ren drives to our destination, whatever it may be. The low clouds, the mountains in the distance, the trees losing their leaves — it looks much like Lake Lyla does this time of year. A few minutes later we exit the freeway and Ren pulls up to the Chihuly Garden and Glass Museum.

Less than a day ago I was on a dock at Lake Lyla for Summer's wedding, my pretend date a man Greta found on a billionaire dating website. And now here I am in Seattle at a glass art installation, primary colors bursting from inside the odd-shaped windowed museum and outside in the gardens.

Life is weird.

I want to stay here all day. I want to go home.

I want to reverse time. I want to speed it up.

We take a seat on a bench in the gardens, the Space Needle spiking up in the distance. The scent of fresh jasmine wafts into my nasal passageways, and tiny sparrows flutter around us.

The bench is long, yet we sit right next to each other, Ren's body touching mine. His body heat is both reassuring and unnerving.

Stay true to your goals, Aut. Don't get carried away — again.

"If you didn't take me here today," I ask, "what would you be doing?"

"I guess I'd be driving back from Lake Lyla to San Francisco, probably on call with Kenny—"

"Who?"

"My business advisor. Helps me find new investment opportunities, identifies advances in technology I need to be aware of, manages my finances. Anyway, drill sergeant Leah would be reciting the upcoming week's agenda. Maybe I'd have a few spare minutes to scroll through social media looking at my favorite map and wine accounts. Maybe the two would converge. A week ago I learned about the wines coming from the Nebbiolo region of northern Italy and the next thing I knew I'd spent three hours and lots of money on a case of wine and a hand-painted map of the region. Anyway, boring, I know." He turns back to gaze up at the Space Needle, the Pacific Northwest's symbol of all that's possible. "And you? What would you be doing right now?"

"Probably a little cleaning, answering emails. Maybe making a stop at Bernie's at some point. The usual. But I'm glad I'm here."

And I am. I'm beginning to see what Leah meant when she called Ren an enigma. Maybe I'd redefine him as incongruous. He doesn't seem to have any "cool" instincts or role models. He's as much into the solar system now as he was as a kid. But he has a confidence that must come from being a billionaire. Yet, with Ren, it's a muted confidence, not showy, not repugnant.

"Want to walk a bit?" he says. "I know a great neighborhood."

"Thought you'd never ask. I need to walk off the pancakes and grilled cheese."

We drive to the Capitol Hill neighborhood and then roam Broadway East, pausing to look in the windows of indie book and record stores.

"Should we head to my place?" Ren says as dusk begins to descend on the Seattle skyline.

"In *San Francisco*?"

"I mean here. I have a place here too."

"You have *another* home? In Seattle?"

"I have several, one of which happens to be in Seattle."

"Exactly how many houses do you have?"

He shrugs, abashed.

"Why so many?"

"I travel a lot for work. Not a fan of hotels."

"Let me guess. Because they're Petri dishes?"

He shrugs and turns away. I've hit a nerve.

"These homes are empty, what, ninety percent of the time?"

"I like having somewhere familiar to land when I travel."

I shake my head. "As my dad would say, some people have more money than sense."

"Savage," Ren says. "But he's probably right."

Ren's Seattle home is a breathtaking penthouse condo in a modern high rise. When we get off the elevator, he pointedly carries my overnight bag to what's clearly a spare bedroom, and I'm not sure whether to be relieved or insulted. Before I can decide, I'm distracted by the view from his living room window of the Space Needle all lit up in the distance. I turn around to see the enormous chef's kitchen, the shininess of the chrome there practically blinding me. There's a man at the large marble island wearing an apron and running dough through a hand-crank pasta machine. Stray flour hovers in the air.

"A chef," I mutter. "Of course you have a chef."

"Believe me, you don't want to taste my cooking."

"Mind if I go freshen up?"

"Be my guest. Around that corner is a powder room."

Ren's "powder room" is larger than my entire bedroom, with textured wallpaper and not one but two sinks. (Why two?) I look at myself in the mirror. My skin is pink from the Washington wind, my hair slightly wavy from the dampness in the Pacific Northwest air. I hate to admit it but this day has invigorated me. Even though my sister's wedding was last night, even though I left my home in a neighboring state almost eight hours ago, I look rested, refreshed and not nearly as emotionally muddled as I'm beginning to feel.

I'm tempted to pull out my phone and call Greta, to tell her about the surprise visit from Ren this morning. The helicopter ride, the grilled cheese, the 150 percent tip, the Tesla ride, not to mention this Architectural Digest-worthy penthouse with its world-class view. I want to tell her how disgusted I am not with Ren, who's entitled to spend his money however he pleases, but with myself for enjoying it all so much when I know there are people suffering, problems to be fixed. Typically, my admiration is reserved for rich people who live decidedly *below* their means.

I hear Ren chatting with the chef and make a mental note to talk to Greta later. I wash my hands and splash water on my face, then use a pump of lotion in the dispenser on the counter, which smells of geranium and almond, to rub into my hands, which always get dry this time of year. I run the bit of excess lotion over my hair to tame the flyaways.

Back out in the kitchen, Ren is cranking the pasta machine under the direction of the chef.

"Want to give it a try?" he asks, after introducing me to the chef.

"Sure." I turn the crank with one hand and guide the linguini with the other, the strands soft and velvety on my fingers.

"Excellent," the chef says. He gently carries the strands to the pot. The pasta is so fresh it only needs about 40 seconds to cook. He drains it and then transfers it into a sauté pan filled with shallots, butter, rosemary, thyme and tomatoes.

When the pasta is plated, we take our dishes to the large round mahogany table.

"Red or white?" the chef says.

Ren looks at me and then back at the chef. "I think we'll pass on wine tonight."

"No, no," I say. "You should have some."

Ren flashes me a comforting, hospitable smile. "It's okay."

"Then I believe my work here is done," the chef says. "Dessert's in the freezer."

If I'm honest with myself, I'm still full from my double-dish breakfast. But nothing is going to keep me from devouring every bite of this meal.

"You did a great job," I say, my mouth full of linguine. "At the wedding yesterday."

"Wasn't hard." He pauses. "Your family is easy to like."

I want to reach over and squeeze his hand. Or get up and stand behind him, wrapping my arms around his neck, and whisper "you're one sexy, nerdy billionaire" in his ear. I want to replay the kiss we shared last night at dinner after the ceremony.

Instead, I glug several gulps of ice water to cool off just like I did earlier at Propeller Kitchen.

"So I know it's gauche but —"

"Gauche? Wait, did my plane take us back to the seventies?"

I laugh. "You're right. Channeling my mom there. She uses that word."

"My grandmother does too," he says, chuckling too. "Sorry to interrupt. You were saying?"

"So, at the risk of being rude, how did this" — I gesture around the room, to the view and the chef's kitchen, all of it — "all start for you?"

"Dungeons and Dragons."

I sit back. "The fantasy...role-playing game?"

For geeky gamers, I want to add, thinking back to the D&D kids I knew growing up.

"The very one."

"I'm going to need a little more."

He grins. "So I got my first summer job — assisting an astrophysicist with research — in high school by putting my D and D experience on my resume, without actually referencing the game."

"More, please."

"I wrote things like" — here, he straightens and deepens his voice to sound more authoritative — "'Meet with colleagues weekly for conflict-resolution practice' and 'Significant experience quickly assessing situations' and 'Collaborate with peers to problem-solve.' Believe it or not, I was hired."

"The professor bought that BS?"

"No," he says. "She saw right through me. She was an avid Dungeons and Dragons player herself. She knew I had no work experience but she told me later that she thought I was clever for trying to parlay gaming into a job."

"Then what?"

"I continued working for her every summer for the next four years. She had a huge grant and paid me quite well, for a student, at least. My parents supported me in college so I was able to save most of the money I earned working for her. I invested some. By the time I was a senior in college, I had a good little chunk of cash."

"Nothing like this, though," I say, gesturing again around his home.

"Not then, no. But right before I graduated, the professor was getting ready to launch a tech company based on a patent that my research assistance helped her get. She asked if I wanted in on the ground floor."

"Did you?"

"I did. I invested every penny I'd earned working for her as well as proceeds from the meager investing I'd started doing."

"And?"

"And less than a year later she sold the company to Eclipse Sciences Corp. and I made my first million."

"Jeez. How old were you?"

"Twenty-one."

"Wow. Good for you. Then what?"

"Eclipse actually hired me. I worked in their R and D department first, then moved over to their investment arm. Got a good salary and continued to do my own investing on the side, all space-related. Eighteen months later, I'd parlayed that first million into ten so I left Eclipse to do my own thing. Great first job, though."

I'll say.

Ren's vision, his science and business skills...it was something to behold. And I'm starting to see that Ren's fortune isn't at all the result of him being money hungry, but rather the byproduct of his enthusiasm for and instincts about a cutting-edge field.

I take the napkin from my lap and place it on the table. "Speaking of *jobs*," I say, clearing my throat. "Let's turn our attention to phase two of Operation Voltaire. Fill me in on your Infinity Symposium. What do I need to know?"

Chapter 15

REN

I'm likely the only person on the planet who likes – maybe even craves – the sharp scent of ammonia.

I'm back at the Inn in Lake Lyla after several days at home in San Francisco where Leah and I grinded out detailed objectives for the Infinity Symposium and where I attended Yom Kippur services. It's now the day before the Infinity Symposium, less than 36 hours before my keynote address. I'm amped up. I want to *convey* something with this speech. I want to garner enthusiasm, commitment, not to mention integrity and lawfulness, when it comes to the exploration and commercialization of space. I want my work and the work of this emerging industry to be for good, to help the environment rather than harm it, to help the unhoused and the sick (who knows what healing minerals await on Pluto or Saturn or planets yet discovered!) rather than to harm anyone, abandon anyone, exclude anyone. I want this work, my legacy, to be for good. My grandmother always says: "Start as you mean to go on." So I want this burgeoning industry to start as a leading movement for positive change, for international collaboration, for beauty, for progress.

I don't think I'd quite realized all of this myself until I started spending time with Autumn. Her constitution seems to be based on how she can help, how she can be a steward for good. It seems that it's not even something that she consciously strives to do or even thinks much about – it's just *who she is*.

I hadn't quite put two and two together in my own life – how I could apply tikun olam, the principle that, like her, I first absorbed at Jewish summer camp, into my life's work. I just knew I want to pursue possibility – not for money, not for glory, but for something I couldn't quite pinpoint. Until recently.

The faint ammonia scent in these rooms at the Inn, the presidential suite, means that they've been cleaned according to my usual strict prescription: double disinfecting of all surfaces from countertops to rugs. But sometimes, like today, it doesn't feel like enough. So I unbag the bleach spray and wipes, which I had delivered to the suite, and embark on my own decontamination ritual. It's already been sanitized by staff so I acknowledge that going one step further is merely to soothe my own personal jitters. I'm aware of what I'm doing. I've talked to enough therapists and doctors to know that I have clinical germaphobia. Hell, it doesn't take a genius to understand that it's the real reason I bought my own plane.

I've been able to work through this personal quirk for the most part and generally it doesn't interfere with my day-to-day life. We all do things to make ourselves feel better, whether it's going for a hard run or repeatedly baking batches of favorite cookie recipes. Soothing rituals are different for everyone. I've come to accept that as long as it's not a *dependency* or a destructive habit like, say, smoking, then I'm going with it. If spraying and wiping and vacuuming calm me down, soothe my brain, take my mind off pressures like an upcoming speech or a beautiful woman that I might otherwise obsess about, then so be it.

After scrubbing the bathroom sink and using a bleach wipe to disinfect the remote controls, the bedroom phone and the light switches, I settle onto the couch to rest for a few minutes. I lay sideways with my socked feet over the arm of the couch and bring the cashmere throw (the same brand I have delivered to every hotel suite I stay at then give to a helpful staff member to enjoy) atop my body. I bring my hands behind my skull, my elbows out in a diamond shape, and gaze out the suite's large picture window. Yellow and white light bounces off the striking amber mountains in the distance. Jagged clouds shape-shift above, pushed quickly eastward by the late September wind.

Despite the comforting aroma of cleaning supplies and the soft weight of the familiar cashmere throw, I feel the burden of aloneness, of feeling foreign. My limbs seem detached from my center, my thoughts too fleeting to harness and settle. It's how I felt much of the time as a child before I met Leah – a feeling of being just outside the inner circle of life. It's a feeling that appears now and then, not so uncomfortable as it once was, but still unrelenting. I've long stopped trying to chase it away. Instead, I acknowledge its recurrence and just hope it doesn't linger too long.

The low murmur of golfers chatting outside and the periodic whack of a club hitting a ball lull me into a late afternoon sleep. When my phone rings, I jolt upright, snapping my eyes open to center myself.

Where am I?

Who am I?

I fumble for my phone, which I locate on the coffee table next to the couch. Caller ID reveals it's Autumn. Seeing that, my heartbeat and breath settle. I remember exactly where I am. Who I am.

I haven't seen her for several days, not since the day I flew her back here to Lake Lyla, first by plane then by helicopter, after our date in Seattle, after which I went home to San Francisco. The day we spent together up in Washington was relaxing. It was easy. And fun. The one strain of the day was showing her to the spare bedroom and then retreating to my own bedroom alone.

God, how I wanted to sweep her into my arms, to trace my fingers over every inch of her body, to lie her gently beneath me, at the very least to relive that manufactured kiss that we shared just the night before at Summer's wedding reception. By most accounts, it would be considered a chaste kiss, barely more than a peck on the lips. But for me, it was acute, weighty, charged.

When we said goodnight in my Seattle hallway, I could have sworn I saw in her eyes a longing, an invitation matching my own desire. But that wasn't why I brought her to Seattle. And I didn't want her to believe that it was. Improbably, I've come to like this woman Leah found for me on a dating site. But our relationship is contract-based and I refuse to take advantage.

"Hello?" I answer, deepening my voice so I don't sound as if I just woke up.

"Hi, Ren. Ready for the big conference?"

I plant my feet on the floor, bring my elbows to my knees and run one hand through my hair. I should have spent the last half hour rehearsing my speech in front of a mirror instead of dozing on the couch. According to Leah, my passion isn't yet coming through, dwarfed by my stiff delivery. It's the same critique she's been giving me since the mock trial unit in our 11th grade Social Studies class. "Getting there," I confess.

"Glad to hear it. Hey, I wanted to talk to you about something...."

Oh crap, is she going to cancel?

I bounce my right knee up and down, aware perhaps for the first time how I've been anticipating spending more time with Autumn. I want to see the wisps of hair escaping her pony tail. I want to smell her floral and earthy scent. I no longer care about fending off eager women or people trying to set me up with friends or sisters or daughters. I don't want her to cancel because *I want to be with her*. I haven't let myself think of what will happen beyond this conference, only grateful that Operation Voltaire still has a Phase Two.

"...something you should know. In the spirit of Yom Kippur, the day of atonement, you know...coming clean and asking forgiveness and all."

"Okay." I strive to even out my tone, like I'm not anticipating the worst.

"You might have noticed that I don't drink much."

I think back to her passing on the high-end wine at Summer's wedding, skipping the mimosa at Propeller Kitchen, declining a glass with homemade pasta. Come to think of it, on Rosh Hashanah, she opted for grape juice. She changed the subject when I told her I'd received the case of award-winning wine from the Nebbiolo region of Italy. "Uh huh."

"Well that's it: I don't drink. I know wine is one of your passions. And I imagine at this conference, like most business conferences, there will be...expectations. Social boozing and all. I just had to tell you in advance that I won't be partaking in that when I'm with you. I hope that won't cause any problems."

"When I'm with you." I settle my bouncing leg and lean back on the couch.

"Oh, hey. I appreciate that. It's okay." My heart slows its rapid pace.

"Really?" She sounds legitimately relieved. "I should have told you when we drew up the contract terms. I mean, some of your colleagues will probably think I'm a wet blanket and that definitely won't be good for your image."

She's still coming.

"Don't give it a second thought. It's fine." My challenge now, I realize, will be to keep my mouth off hers. I've tasted her once and it wasn't enough.

Silence.

"Do you, uh, want to talk more about it?" I ask.

"Um, I didn't, you know, hit 'rock bottom' or anything. It never reached the level of 'addiction.' But a couple of years ago, I realized not only do I not like how I feel when I drink, but I don't like who I *am*."

"Who you are....?" I can't imagine her being anything other than soft, cheerful.

"When I drink, I do things like gossip. I make comments that are not-so-thinly-veiled insults. And I...basically, I become an asshole."

I'm quiet because I simply cannot picture it.

"Once, after two glasses of wine," she continues, "I told a friend — a good friend — that her new shirt did a great job covering her back fat."

I wince. But then I look over and see the bag of cleaning supplies I had delivered here and remember that we all have parts of ourselves that are odd, that are different, that we're not proud of. The key, my grandmother always told me, is to "own yourself." Once you do, you have more compassion for yourself and for others.

"Hey, Autumn," I say softly. "I'm just glad you'll be there."

"Of course, I'll be there," she says, and I can practically see the adorable way her cheeks bunch when she smiles. "It's part of our contract, *hon*."

"Can I ask you something?" I say to Leah, who's come to my suite to help me run through the keynote address for the 700th time. She's wearing sweats and a t-shirt that says, "Butch, please" across the front.

"Yup."

"Why'd you pick Autumn?"

She puts down the iPad she's been using to highlight in yellow the words I should emphasize when giving the speech. "*You* picked Autumn. As with most things — the tile for your bathroom remodel, the candidates for a new position in your company — I simply narrowed it down to three."

I stare back, not blinking, stone-faced. It's a mutual tactic we use that means, "Don't buy it. Try again."

She turns sideways on the couch and tucks her legs underneath her. "Okay. Yes, technically I narrowed it to three but I knew you'd pick Autumn."

I nod, satisfied. "And why did you set it up that way?"

"I just had a feeling she'd be the right person...for the job."

I think about Greta and how she apparently picked *me* because of the way the planets and stars were aligning in the sublunar world. Given my own obsession with celestial bodies, who am I to argue with that method? "Can you elaborate?"

Leah leans an elbow on the back of the couch. "It started with her photo. It was a candid. Clearly not a professional headshot or photoshopped."

Because Greta submitted a photo of Autumn from her own phone without Autumn even knowing.

"And that showed me," Leah continues, "that she wasn't the type to try too hard, unlike so many others on Billionaire Rendezvous."

"What else?"

"Her profile narrative struck me as authentic, again not trying too hard, not eager to show that she was interested in money and also not trying to show that she *wasn't* interested in money. Rather, it focused on her personal qualities — passionate, devoted — rather than achievements."

Again, Greta.

"Anything else?" I'm searching for something but I'm not sure what it is.

Leah brings a finger to her chin, looks to the ceiling, as if she's confused by the question. But then she looks back at me. "Why did you introduce me and Samantha?"

I met Samantha several years ago when she was the office manager for my dentist. I required two root canals and a filling in a single year so I visited that office frequently then. Samantha and I had a quick, easy rapport. One of the first times we spoke she made reference to having broken up with a girlfriend. A few months later, when my dental issues were finally resolving, even though I didn't really *know* Samantha, I asked if she was willing to be set up. I just had a sense she was right for Leah. "Just a gut feeling that you two would hit it off," I say to Leah.

It turned out I was right. After their second date, she and Samantha were inseparable.

Leah places her index finger on the tip of her nose. "Bingo."

"Wait — what?" I toss my papers aside.

"Don't be mad."

Mad? How could I be mad that she orchestrated me meeting someone as fun, as refreshing as Autumn? I'm just....

"God, I'm dumb," I say.

"No, not dumb. Just dense. And I truly do believe that having someone by your side for the Infinity Symposium is going to serve as a good deterrent."

"Why Autumn, though?" Speaking her name is a candy on my tongue.

She scoots towards me. "I've known you since we were kids. I know you say you're not interested in a long-term relationship. That's fine. But if you're going to need a date for something, why not go with someone who'll be good for you? Someone real, someone outside your normal sphere, someone with substance, who probably couldn't care less about your deals and your ascension in the space industry."

"You could tell all that about Autumn from a Billionaire Rendezvous profile? One she didn't even write?"

Leah turns back around, grabbing her tablet and a stack of folders from the coffee table, ready to return to the tasks at hand. "When are you going to realize that, yes, I'm that good?"

Chapter 16

AUTUMN

So far so good.

We're onto Phase Two of Operation Voltaire. It's the first night of Ren's conference, a celebratory gala welcoming attendees before several days of jam-packed seminars and panels and the all-important keynote address that begin tomorrow.

I arrived at the Inn a couple of hours ago, meeting Ren in his suite (the presidential suite, previously occupied by A-list visitors to Lake Lyla such as LeBron James and Jennifer Lawrence) to get ready so that we'd arrive to the ballroom arm-in-arm, as the believable couple Ren needs us to be. I've spent my whole life coming to the Inn – for pre-graduation brunches, to work as a golf caddy during high school summers, for weddings and bar and bat mitzvahs. But I've never set foot in the presidential suite before.

Ren's accommodations here include more square footage than my parents' entire house, including two ginormous bedrooms and separate living and dining rooms. It's decorated in a hip Art Deco-meets-lodge vibe, all dark wood with black and white accents. When I got here, Leah was in the midst of helping Ren sort out which tux (*which* tux! choices!) to wear, while simultaneously reciting personal facts about VIP conference attendees so that he'd be better able to charm and make connections.

Not that anyone asked me but her ferocious prep is probably unnecessary. Ren is charming all on his own, just as he is. Exhibit A: my sisters have been continually texting me since the wedding a couple of weeks ago, asking when they'll get to see him again. And despite the fact that Ren is nothing like my normal "type," I confessed to myself earlier today how excited I've been to spend these next few days with him, ever since the surprise date in Seattle a week ago.

I haven't known Ren long, and our spending time together is by an arrangement with strict parameters. But I've come to find him endearingly goofy, effortlessly sexy. The first half of that night in Seattle, I stared at the ceiling of his spare bedroom, hornier than I'd been in months, wondering if — hoping! — he'd knock softly on my door and invite himself in for a continuation of our first kiss. When he didn't, I spent the second half of the night wondering what would happen if *I* knocked on *his* door. But I suppose we're both too principled to do something so outside the bounds of our contract. After all, I know his reasons for Operation Voltaire and he knows mine.

Here, in the presidential suite, I have my own room once again, this time to change out of my skinny jeans into my one and only dress suitable for black-tie attire. After pulling off my eyeglasses (which I forego for tonight since there's almost zero chance anyone here will confuse me with Winter), slipping on my shoes and moving a few items from my big purse into my small clutch, I return to the suite's living room where Ren and Leah are still discussing who he should make an effort to speak to, who he needs to impress.

When Ren sees me, his jaw goes slack, so much so that Leah turns around to see what's stunned him. She breaks into an approving grin when she discovers it's me.

"Autumn," she says, "you look—"

"— exquisite," Ren finishes her thought.

His eyes are piercing, making me feel as if he sees right through my cranberry velvet dress, staring directly at my completely naked body. I feel myself blush, not from embarrassment but from the fact that I'm imagining *him* unclothed as well. I think of that kiss at Summer's wedding, soft and powerful at the same time. Was it our first kiss...or our only kiss?

Focus, Autie. You need to do as good a job fulfilling your *end of Operation Voltaire as he did at his.*

Leah snaps her fingers to regain Ren's attention and completes her final instructions.

"Oh, and after all that," she concludes, "you two kids try to have some fun."

Ren and I leave the suite and make our way downstairs to the ballroom, our bodies separated by mere inches even though the hallways are wide. I hold my small purse with two hands because if I don't, one of my palms might go rogue and swipe slowly along Ren's back side.

I've never seen the ballroom so spectacular. The normally staid room has been transformed into a space-themed extravaganza, complete with an enormous, shiny hanging solar system and simulated stars. The 150 or so guests mill about in fashion-forward designer clothing suitable for the Oscars or the Met Gala.

It doesn't take long for me to see why Ren needed a decoy date for this conference. As we mingle with executives, scientists and academics, I field countless pointed stares, some reproving, some evaluative. And once again, I begin to see

Ren in a new light. Clearly in his element, he has equally high-level conversations with a former Defense Secretary, the founder of an airline, and a female supermodel, the date of a 20-something tech bro.

Though his keynote address won't take place until tomorrow, he's tasked with standing at a podium on risers at the front of the room to formally welcome all guests to the symposium and to tonight's gala. When Leah gives him the signal that it's time, I watch him walk to the mic with self-possession and ease. When he speaks, his face projected onto a big screen, I can't help but feel the pride of proximity, akin to how I felt when Summer said her heartfelt vows to Cole or how I felt when my brother Colin, a pianist, performed in front of 3,000 people at the legendary Fox Theater in Oakland.

When Ren returns to our table, the applause of the ballroom as the soundtrack, I place my hand over his. "Great job, *babe*." It isn't until he replies, "Thanks, *hon*," that I realize that the term of endearment had inadvertently slipped from my mouth and had not been sarcastic at all.

After a meal of kale salad with persimmons, ravioli with pumpkin brown butter sauce, and chocolate cake with pomegranate compote, the dinner portion of the evening winds down. Half of our table gets up to enjoy casino-themed events in the neighboring room.

"Am I doing okay?" I whisper.

"Flawless," he says, his breath thick in my ear. I shiver. "Want to step outside for a few minutes?"

I nod, and he gets up and slowly pulls my chair back so I can rise in a lady-like fashion. We make our way through the ballroom toward a nearby terrace, several people stopping him along the way, shaking his hand, saying how they're looking forward to hearing his address tomorrow.

Out on the terrace, the sky is so brilliant it looks almost fake, with deep purple clouds and a low, pearly moon. We lean against the railing and gaze up in silence.

"There's so much to explore out there," Ren says wistfully. Then he turns his attention back here, to this moment, to the two of us.

"You're breathtaking in that dress. So simple, so elegant."

"Thanks. I don't have fancy diamonds or pearls to embellish it like I've seen others wearing in that ballroom."

"Jewelry would only detract from the effect."

There's not a soul out here to overhear us, no one he needs to prove our relationship to.

"It's weird mingling with all these gazillionaires," I add. "It's all so outside my normal realm. I see there's a whole parallel world existing alongside my regular life. You're good with all of this, Ren. Really in your element." I take a step closer to him.

A boisterous cheer erupts from the casino room.

"By the way, I know that Operation Voltaire," I whisper, "will soon end."

His face darkens in the moonlight.

"But I'm wondering if there could be some kind of...addendum."

I'm not breaking the promise to myself to stay uncoupled. This is just a small extension of our contract.

He tilts his head and smiles. "How so?"

I interlock the fingers of both my hands to curb the urge to unbutton his tuxedo jacket and rest them on his chest. "There's a fundraiser that I'm helping to organize." I look around the Inn tonight with its fancy trappings that probably cost more than the amount I'll need to raise. I gesture back to the ballroom. "It'll be nothing like this," I say with a light smirk. "It's in a rec center, a spaghetti feed to raise money for someone who needs medication that insurance won't cover. I realized after we established the terms of Operation Voltaire that it'll really only work if it's not a one-off. Some of my family will be at the fundraiser, which'll make our relationship more believable and also –"

"—say no more. I'm in."

"I haven't even told you when it is. You'll have to come back up here from the Bay Area...."

"Doesn't matter. I'd love to come. I'll make it work."

We turn to face each other head on, our bodies suddenly like magnets that can't pull apart.

"Should I draw up a formal addition to our contract?"

He laughs, his voice low. "Not necessary. I'll be there."

Wordlessly, we turn and head back into the ballroom, which, we discover, has all but emptied out.

"Should we move onto the blackjack tables so you can mingle more?" I ask.

Ren grasps my hand and leads me away from the casino room. "Let's go."

His steps are hurried but purposeful, and it feels as if we're having a whole conversation. But we're silent, communicating our mutual desire in body language, our torsos rubbing against each other with each hasty step. We reenter the presidential suite and discover the hotel has delivered a bottle of port and chocolate-dipped dried apricots. We dart right past it all, practically running through the living room that's quadruple the size of my own on our way to his bedroom.

Finally we stop.

We look to the bed and then to each other. I give Ren the slightest of nods and that's all he needs. He cups his hands gently around the back of my skull, his thumbs on my jawline. His eyes are dewy, yet filled with fire.

I want him. Badly. But I wait.

He brings his lips to my forehead, so lightly I'm not even sure that we've actually touched. Can he feel my shudder?

When he releases, I tilt my chin up. We're both breathing heavy. I want his mouth on mine. I almost say it out loud. Almost beg. But he already knows it. Rather than oblige, he moves his lips to one cheek, then slowly to the other, his warm, minty breath right under my nose.

I can't wait any longer.

Now, I clasp his face between my hands. I'm panting. The only way to catch my breath is to stifle it completely by kissing him.

In response, he moans into my mouth. The sound and the wetness of his tongue meeting mine creates a slickness between my legs.

"Why are we doing this?" I say, threading my fingers through his hair, as soft as fine cashmere. "No one's watching."

His hands travel down my neck to my shoulders. He turns me around so I'm facing away from him. Slowly — so slowly the waiting becomes almost painful — he unzips my gown, vertebra by vertebra, making me shiver more with each inch. By the time he turns me back around to face him, my legs are weak and I don't know how much longer I can stand.

With two index fingers, he tenderly pushes the straps of the gown down and the entire dress drops to the floor. "It's just you and me," he confirms, grinning wickedly.

He kisses me powerfully while expertly unhooking my strapless bra. I feel our noses touch, our teeth. When my chest is bare, he pulls back, looking me in the eyes as he runs his thumbs over my nipples with the slightest touch.

A feral sound erupts from deep within me. I have never felt so aroused in my life. His touch is like music. The slightest movement will send me over the edge.

But it's too soon.

I pull back.

I can't look at his eyes or I may explode. Instead, I watch my hands as they unbuckle his belt, unzip his pants and grab him. I feel different than I have with any man and I sense this is a once-in-a-lifetime connection. While every one of my nerve endings is on fire, I work to memorize everything — every breath, every touch. I must capture this feeling because this, what's happening between me and Ren, was never in the plan and will likely never happen again.

"Oh God," he whispers.

A nanosecond later, we're on the bed, clutching, squeezing, licking, stroking. I want to feast on him, be enveloped by him.

"You're more beautiful than Saturn," he pants.

I trace my fingers over his pecs. "What?"

"The most spectacular planet." His words come in puffs and groans. "Its ringlets, its Titan moon, its lakes and dark terrain."

Hovering over me, he raises my arms over my head and kisses me so intensely I feel as if I'm being swallowed. I want to be swallowed.

He moves his mouth down my torso, licking my nipples while at the same time his hand finds my very center. As he circles me with an index finger, his mouth moves to my other nipple. I feel myself turning inside out and I cannot wait, cannot stop it. My hips raise and lower on their own without my consent. My mind is empty. I cannot think. I can only feel. Within seconds, I'm arching, shuddering, moaning. I feel my eyes nearly roll back inside my skull.

My body is still quivering as I hear Ren ripping open protection. Once it's on, I grab his biceps and pull him on top of me. Then I reach down and place him between my legs.

"Oh God," he says for the second time as he slides inside me.

Again, we move together and it feels as if we've done this before, in my imagination, in my dreams.

Chapter 17

REN

A loud snore awakens me. I open my eyes and roll my head to the side. Sun beams in through the window. In our haste to get naked, I never closed the blinds and now it shines right onto Autumn as she continues to snore, a dissonant, irregular snoring kind of sound that's in stark contrast to how she looks in this moment. The sunlight bathes her in an otherworldly glow, her hair shines, chestnut streaks glimmering. The sheet drifting off her shoulder exposes the luscious curve of her breast. I'd never really believed in a post-coital or morning-after glow. But right now I'm proved wrong, experiencing it for the first time. The harshness of her snoring cannot take away from Autumn's beauty.

I return my gaze back up to the ceiling, wondering what this new...development means. Last night was as fiery and surprising as it was inevitable, even, somehow, familiar. Despite the fact that relationships haven't been my priority and, as a result, haven't been long lasting, I've had some pretty excellent sex in my day, starting with losing my virginity at 19 to a gorgeous 35-year-old divorcee I met at a bar while on a post-high school Europe trip.

But last night was like nothing I've ever experienced. "Epic" is so overused these days as to diminish its impact, but epic is an apt descriptor for what I experienced with Autumn. It was passionate, tender, explosive, and...natural. It was as if, in merging our bodies, layers of deep-seated loneliness peeled from my body, from my spirit, leaving me utterly exposed, laid bare. And to my shock, I was content, unafraid. I thought this feeling was make-believe, something only felt in rom com movies like Pretty Woman. The closest I've come to that kind of euphoria was earning my first million. But even that pales in comparison to last night.

Autumn inhales deeply with an accompanying snort, so loud it wakes her. She has that confused look of waking up somewhere unfamiliar, but then she turns, sees me staring, and I might burst from the genuine expression of delight that washes over her.

"You snore like an eighty-year-old man with emphysema."

"I know," she says lazily. She stretches her arms over her head and reaches her toes as far as she can in the other direction. "What time is it?"

I pick up my phone, which is resting on the side table. "Nine-fifteen."

She raises up her torso and leans back onto her forearms. "Don't you need to be downstairs? For the conference?"

Her concern warms me. I shake my head. "The program doesn't begin until lunchtime today. The organizers planned it that way, figuring everyone would need a few extra hours this morning after last night's festivities."

She leans over the side of the bed and grabs her own phone, which, like her dress and panties, is on the floor next to the bed. With a thumb, she scrolls through a handful of texts. Her nails are painted a sexy dark red. She hovers on one message and then looks over at me.

"This isn't part of Operation Voltaire, but do you have any interest in hanging out with my sisters and a couple of friends this morning at The Book Mark?"

"The Book Mark?"

"It's a cafe-bookstore owned by Jules's family. Remember Summer's best friend?"

"You had me at cafe."

We throw on our clothes, a bit shyly in the harsh morning light, and Autumn packs up her overnight bag.

"What's all this stuff?" She points to the cleaning supplies in the corner of the bedroom.

I feel a burning in my chest.

I could lie. I could deflect. I could say it's Leah's stuff or that the hotel's housekeeping forgot it there. I've done all those things in the past. But Autumn is different. And I feel different when I'm with Autumn. She revealed to me why she no longer drinks. So, in the spirit of Yom Kippur, I own up too.

"Cleaning, like obsessive, deep sanitizing...I guess you could say it's a hobby of mine?"

Without reaction, she continues packing up her things. Her expression reveals neither disgust or amusement. It's an invitation, I understand, to continue.

I run a hand through my hair. "Yeah, so I guess you could say I'm a bit of a germaphobe. When I stay in hotels, I do my own disinfecting."

"I see."

I lean my head to the right. "Those sheets we slept on—"

"—among other things," Autumn says, with a provocative grin, pulling her hair into that messy bun I love.

"Yeah, I bring my own sheets to hotels."

She sucks her lower lip underneath her teeth. "I see," she repeats, realization dawning on her. "The private plane, the many homes...."

This is when she realizes I'm a complete freak.

I nod.

"Okay," she says, as if an uninteresting mystery has been solved. "Ready to go?"

The air inside The Book Mark is dense and enveloping, a welcome contrast to the wind whipping outside, shifting leaves and scattering discarded scraps of paper here and there along the sidewalk. The scent of espresso is strong, rivaling the allure of Bernie's.

Jules is at the checkout counter, thoroughly engrossed in a book titled "PEEPS," with a purplish hue and an RV on its cover.

"Hey, Jules," Autumn says.

"Hi, Autie." Jules says, lifting her gaze from the pages. Then she notices me. "Oh, hi again, Ren. Head on back. Your sisters already have a table. I'll be back there in a minute."

We walk through the store, its colorful tables and shelves inviting. Autumn stops in front of a table devoted to science fiction. "Ooh," she says, picking up a novel with a silver spaceship on the cover.

"Science fiction, huh?" I say.

"A little, but also fantasy. I love the world-building."

"Opposites really do attract."

"Why? What kind of books do you like?"

I lean in and whisper. "Rom coms."

"Seriously?"

"A good story is a good story. I just get in the mood once in a while for some fun banter, the assurance of a happily ever after. I read them on an e-reader so no one can razz me. No one except Leah, of course, who manages my Amazon account."

She laughs. "I'm not surprised. After all, you seem to love Pretty Woman *almost* as much as I do."

I feel lighter after unburdening myself – about my disinfecting rituals, about my love of rom coms, atypical for my gender. We stroll to nearby tables covered in colorful displays. I pick up a biography of Winston Churchill from the new releases table, while Autumn homes in on a beginners book about playing guitar. She flips through it, revealing diagrams and musical staff notes. "I've been teaching myself with online videos, but I haven't yet seen a reference book like this."

"Let me get it for you."

"What? No, no, I wasn't fishing."

"Of course you weren't." Autumn matches my grandmother in her utter disinterest in my net worth and I'm beginning to see that her attitude has enabled me to be more *me* around her. Trying to live up to someone's expectations of what a billionaire should be is a large part of what's kept me from seeking a relationship. There's none of that with Autumn. "But," I counter in a hushed tone, "what good is it being a billionaire if you can't buy your fake girlfriend a book?"

She shuts the book and tucks it under her arm. "Thanks, *hon*."

"Aut! We have to stop meeting like this."

We both turn around to see Noah, her colleague, the man who she introduced me to at Rosh Hashanah services.

"Oh, hi, Noah."

He gives me a clipped, we've-met-before nod and I return it. "What are you up to?" he says.

"Meeting people for coffee. You?"

He holds up a stack of books, among them a "Best Hiking Trails in the West" guide and a biography of Melinda Gates.

Now it's me who's reminded that Autumn and I live in different worlds. Hers, the small town where she's surrounded by loved ones and longtime friends and where she can pursue her philanthropic ambitions in her down time. Mine, the corporate world, a world of lawyers, venture capitalists and for-profit scientists, peppered with my antisocial hobbies of cartography and wine.

We yet haven't discussed what last night means, whether our sleeping together voids our contract or somehow enhances it.

After saying goodbye to Noah, we continue to the back of the store, to the cafe area, where it smells not only of espresso but also of cinnamon and cranberry oatmeal muffins, still warm from the oven according to a "Today's Special" sign at the counter.

Summer, Winter and Greta are at a table near the back window. I know many people confuse Autumn and Winter but I see how different they are. Autumn's whole vibe is softer than Winter's. Winter's hair is a bit darker and although she has the same large, pretty teeth, Autumn's lower teeth are slightly less straight. And today, anyway, Autumn has that distinct after-sex glow. I wonder if anyone else here can see it.

We order coffees at the counter and join the table, Jules settling in right behind us. I note their welcoming smiles, their willingness to squish an extra person, a man no less, at the small table. Greta gives me a knowing but supportive look. It's all such a contrast to any sort of comparable event in my circles, the no-nonsense demeanor of my colleagues, the moneyed expectations.

"Sum, how was your honeymoon?" Greta asks.

"Too short!"

Autumn leans over and explains to me that Summer works for the school district and wasn't able to take more than a few days off work given that it's the beginning of the school year.

"But it was great," Summer says. "We went down to—"

In my pocket, my phone buzzes with the arrival of a text. I pull it out half-way out and see it's from Kenny.

"CALL ME."

I take my first sip of coffee and check the time. I flash my phone to Autumn. "Need to take this. And even though we just got here, now that I am looking at the time, I've got to get ready for today's program."

She nods. "Just confirming," she whispers, "nothing for me today, right? Next event for me is tomorrow?"

"Yup." I pick up her guitar instruction book and tilt it back and forth. "This'll be up front waiting for you."

Chapter 18

AUTUMN

When Ren places his large, warm hand on my thigh under the table, it's like a live wire has touched me.

We're at the Book Mark hanging out with Summer, Jules, Winter and Greta, hearing about Summer's short but sweet honeymoon. The first few minutes here at this table were a weird mishmash of my old and my new lives – my old life with my sisters and girlfriends and my new life, a life that began with a contract and has morphed into one of an unexpected kinship and, as of last night, toe-curling sex.

The skin between my nose and my upper lip is raw from Ren's scruff rubbing my face when we kissed, deep and longing kisses. My legs muscles are weak, my back tired from arching involuntarily in pleasure. I'm both exhausted and wired from last night and there's been zero time to process what it all means. We'd accounted for only the mildest of PDA in our contract, but had never ever imagined having *sex* given that the whole idea of this mutually beneficial contract was to further our shared goal to *not* be in relationships.

Snippets of words that Summer is saying – ocean, champagne and relaxing – drift into my brain, but I'm not really here. Part of me wishes I was at Bernie's, with just Ren, so we could sort this out, write things down, devise new contract terms. And if not at Bernie's with Ren, I wish I was at my apartment by myself with my second-hand guitar under tucked against my torso, my fingers brushing the metal of the strings, the vibrational sounds likely off-key or at least too slow to resemble any type of actual song. But it would at least be something to have all to myself.

Now, though, his hand is on my thigh, creating an instant portal back to right now, to this moment. He leans over and shows me his phone with a message from his business advisor. He must be good, this Kenny guy, because Ren is a billionaire and, from everything I witnessed last night at the gala, is the darling of the space industry.

Ren holds up the guitar book that he's sweetly buying for me as he says his goodbyes and leaves to make his call and prepare for the first real day of the conference. As he walks away, I fixate on the broadness of his body. Something like a fever washes over me as I remember that same body on top of me, under me, next to me last night, and I hope no one else notices my body temperature rising.

I observe two women standing at the memoir section, both of whom stare at Ren as he passes, following his every move with their heads. And when he's out of sight, they look at each other and giggle, fanning their faces with their hands to indicate that he is hot.

If you only knew, I think, recalling the expert ways he touched me last night. And these women are hot for Ren without even knowing that he's also a billionaire.

I force my attention back to the table and Greta's eyes meet mine. Greta, the only person who knows the nature of – or should I say the *origin* of? – my relationship with Ren. That it's a farce, that it's temporary, that it's by agreement.

Her look is knowing, piercing. She must sense the change in status because her gaze morphs and becomes questioning, softening. After all, she also knows that the very reason for our agreement is that I insisted it's time for me to be an individual, to separate from my sisters, to stop the years-long train of boyfriend after boyfriend. This is still my mission, though I'm pushing it aside until after Operation Voltaire is complete.

"*Well?*" Winter says, her espresso breath hot on my right cheek.

"Sorry, what?"

All four of them – not just Greta – are now staring at me. It's clear I've been stuck inside my own head, missing the conversation.

"Tell us how things are going with *Ren*," she says.

"Quite a snack," Jules says.

Summer laughs. "I'm a married woman now but I have to agree. He gives new meaning to dark and handsome."

"He's Jewish too," I add for some inexplicable reason.

"No way!" Winter says.

"We actually met" – I look slyly at Greta – "at synagogue at Rosh Hashanah services. Just like us, his mom is Jewish. And his maternal grandmother had a large hand in raising him. He even went to Jewish camp."

"Something else about your boyfriend?" Jules pipes up. "He's loaded."

"What do you mean?" Summer asks.

"I've seen his picture before in Magnate magazine. It's a publication we recently started carrying here at the store. From what I read, he's a legit pioneer, a 'visionary,'" she makes air quotes, "in the private space industry. Also a high-end map collector. And owns some of the most expensive wines out there — takes 'wine club' to a whole other level."

Winter places her palms on the edge of the table and straightens her arms. "Our Autie, on every nonprofit organization's wish list of employees, queen of fundraisers and bake sales for the smallest of causes...dating a *billionaire*!"

"Kind of gross, right?" I say.

Summer puts down her coffee. "What do you mean by that?"

I shake my head slightly. "When I think of every bit of good that can be done with money like that...." I let the thought drift. I don't mention the helicopter ride to his private jet, the multiple homes, the chefs.

"Cinder-fucking-rella," Winter says, and everyone laughs at her pitch perfect nod to the iconic Pretty Woman line.

"Do you *like* him?" Greta says, grounding the conversation.

I shift in my seat, tempted to spew about last night, how satiated I feel, how it was as if we'd been together many times before.

"I do," I murmur before I can moderate my words.

Shit. I do.

What about my commitment to living as a single person? To understand myself as an individual?

I made a pledge to finally figure out who I am. If I ditch on myself after this first and only try, then what does that say about me?

I tip my chair back onto its rear legs in an effort to distance myself from the inquiries, the probing looks of my sisters and friends. I lean a little too far and almost lose my balance, almost tumble down until Winter, my identical sister, reaches her arm out to steady me.

Chapter 19

REN

"What's with the all-caps text?" I ask Kenny as I drive back to the Inn from The Book Mark.

"We fucked 'em, Ren! Thanks to some connections I've been massaging, we got into the Lunula deal without those losers at DRM Industries knowing a thing about it. They'll be chasing us into the next millennium!"

"Okay."

"Christ, I'd expect more enthusiasm from you on this. It took some clever maneuvering, months of work."

The windows of my Prius are rolled down a few inches to let the blustery air filter into the car to help wake me up. I was only able to have a few gulps of coffee, not enough to counteract the very little sleep I got last night with Autumn there next to me, unexpected yet somehow inescapable, and glorious. I need to get a grip, to pause the images of her bare calves, her stomach, her neck flitting through my mind. The heart of the Infinity Symposium begins today.

"Good work," I say, though my mind is on Autumn, not the Lunula deal, a multi-million dollar opportunity that seems oddly unimportant compared to, say, a woman whose insurance won't cover life-saving medication.

"You outside? I hear wind."

I roll up two of the four windows. "In my car."

"Ren, dude. Conference starts in less than *two hours*. Why aren't you there networking? Or at the very least rehearsing your keynote?"

Because Autumn invited me to spend more time with her this morning.

"Kenny, you worry too much."

"Where are you driving from?"

"Coffee. With a friend."

"Jesus, Ren. Not *that woman* you went to some wedding with...."

That woman. "What the hell, Kenny? Are you Bill Clinton now?"

"She should be vetted!"

"What?"

"It's not just that she could be a gold digger looking for a sugar daddy because of course there's that. But what about corporate espionage? You keeping your phone and computer out of her reach?"

I silently pound a fist against the steering wheel. I want to tell Kenny that Autumn was all Leah's idea. Leah, who I trust as much as anyone in the world, as much as my grandmother, who has nothing but my best interests at heart. But now Autumn has become more than just an ornament or a decoy.

"She's not a gold digger," I spit out between gritted teeth.

But how do I know?

I hate that Kenny plants a sliver of doubt.

"To be frank," I continue, "I think she finds my financial status a turn *off*. Finds my personal plane, multiple homes – unsettling, maybe even repulsive. It's refreshing."

"You've taken her on the *plane*?"

"Kenny, why did you want to speak with me?"

"Not trying to be a douche, here, but as your business advisor, it's my job to look out for your interests. Be careful. But back to the matter at hand: we've been approached about an opportunity, a chance for a majority stake in Galaquarry, the premiere manufacturer of spectrometers."

I feel the familiar buzz in my chest when something exclusive, cutting-edge and potentially lucrative is placed before me. "Go on."

"They're looking to merge with an aerospace nano-mining company. Founded by a UC Berkeley chemist. Woman was nominated for a Nobel."

"And they need me for?"

"Funds, of course."

"Of course." I take a right and travel the Ponderosa pine-lined road toward the Inn. I recall the night I just spent with Autumn, how before I leaned in for our first *real* kiss, not one just for show at a wedding reception, we talked about her emerging interest in the repatriation of Indigenous property, both cultural property and actual land. "How, exactly, will this merger, this investment benefit humanity?" I think of refugees, diseases that urgently need cures, countries that don't have clean water.

"Benefit huma—? The fuck does that have to do with anything? It's a chance for you to make a boatload off of someone else's idea."

"And for *you* to make a boatload too, given that you receive a hefty cut of every deal you bring to me."

"Is this news? That's how this has worked for more than a decade. What, exactly, is going on with you, Ren?"

I expel air slowly, like I'm blowing out a single birthday candle. "How much they looking for?"

"I'll text the figures and a PDF of their proposal. Take a look and call me this evening after the conference."

I park at the Inn but instead of heading inside to the presidential suite, I remain outdoors, meandering around to the back. "What's the rush?"

"The *rush?* Jesus, Ren, you know the rush. If we don't sign on immediately they'll go to someone else."

I pause near the first hole of the golf course. Amidst Kenny's blathering is the trickle of water. Glancing to my left, I notice a shallow creek.

"Do you want Chuck Harger to get it instead of you, Ren? Or worse, that loony prick Elon Musk?"

Kenny is simply espousing what has long been my world view: that resources are scarce, that there's a finite pie of money, of luck, of opportunity. But I'm no longer sure that's actually the case.

"Assuming I *want* to invest in this project for a company that will extract minerals from other planets and doesn't do anything for *people*, why wouldn't they want money from me *and* others? Can't it be a win-win-win for all of us?"

"Returns would be diluted!"

"So we'd make, what, *twenty* million instead of thirty?"

A pause. "Something like that."

I sit on a boulder on the bank of the creek, the smoky scent of a fireplace from the Inn hovers in the air, making me feel both warm and cold at the same time. A slice of morning moon shines in the sky and, as always when I contemplate the cosmos, I grasp how small we are amidst earth and space. A woodpecker taps at the bark of a tree next to me and an owl blares like a metronome nearby.

"You in the goddamn wilderness now?" Kenny says, his tone bordering on exasperation.

"Just outside the Inn. There's a creek here."

"Jesus, Ren, can you go inside, review the speech, and get down to the ballroom to greet people before the luncheon program starts? This is *your* conference. You, me, Leah, we've all been working towards this – and everything that may result from it – for months."

"You're right. Talk later." I hang up, and stay planted on the boulder.

Chapter 20

AUTUMN

Normally populated by sweaty teens playing pick-up basketball, the North Shore rec hall this evening is swimming in the scent of basil and garlic, and it hits me as soon as I set foot inside. Volunteers are milling about, hanging hand-drawn signs on butcher paper, lacing streamers over the backs of metal chairs. But my spidey sense tells me that, despite the seeming flurry of activity, this is an unorganized effort. I check the time – there are fewer than 90 minutes to whip this event into shape. I'm not the official host of this fundraiser, which is raising money for Madeline, a 35-year-old mom of two, who requires pricey treatment for a rare pulmonary disease. A single pill, which Madeline requires seven days a week, costs $100. The treatment, an off-label use for cystic fibrosis meds, isn't covered by health insurance. Madeline's cousin, who's a friend of a friend, asked me several weeks ago to help manage the event. I step atop one of the metal chairs.

Curling my lips and tongue, I produce loudest whistle I can. Instantly the disorganized buzz quiets as everyone freezes and looks up at me, the apparent crazy lady standing on a chair.

The only sound now is Kanye blasting from the industrial kitchen in the neighboring room.

I channel Winter, the bossy triplet.

"Hi, everyone. My name is Autumn Sky and Madeline's family asked me to organize tonight's event. Thanks for helping to make this spaghetti feed fundraiser a success. Let's make sure we've got everything perfect when guests come. Join me over here to sort out what still needs to be done and what role each of us should have." I start ticking items off with my fingers. "We've got ticketing and cashiering, decorations, cooks, food servers, silent auction set-up, cleanup crew. So gather around."

I step down and begin handing out assignments to the twenty or so volunteers and get everything rolling. Long ago, I learned to approach event preparation like a recipe: start with whatever will take the longest and whatever needs to be fully complete before the next step can begin. And move on from there.

Once everyone heads off to their assignments, I feel a light tap on my shoulder. I turn and there's Ren. He's wearing a pale pink t-shirt and the no-name jeans we bought together a few weeks ago at Barnard's, the ones that cling to his lower half in all the right places, a visual reminder of his muscular, hairy legs. My skin buzzes just being near him for the first time in 10 days. We were last together for the final cocktail party of the Infinity Symposium, which Ren deemed an unprecedented success. Not only does he now have deals in the works with AstroSat and SolarZ, two key startups he was able to cultivate without distraction at the conference, but Ren's keynote address received a standing ovation and was described by an industry publication as "forward-thinking and clever, a commanding reminder that space holds both promise and responsibility, fortune and obligation."

Before he checked out of the Inn's presidential suite, we went upstairs to "use" the bed one last time, another explosive round of sex that raises my body temperature every time I think about it, which is a lot. The other day at work, Noah asked if he should open the window to let some air in because he noticed my cheeks were turning crimson.

Since that last day at the conference, Ren has been in San Francisco working furiously on solidifying those deals. We've FaceTimed once or twice, planning the addendum, the final phase of Operation Voltaire — this rec center fundraiser — and analyzing Julia Roberts's new film, which he saw last weekend with Leah and Samantha and I saw with my sisters. When I mentioned how helpful the guitar instruction book he got me was, he asked me to demonstrate my new skills. I'm no natural but surprisingly my rendition of Hotel California wasn't awful.

Something we *haven't* done is discuss what happens after Operation Voltaire officially ends tonight. Our contract — the original two events and this fundraiser — has protected us. Having strict parameters has enabled us to avoid facing the implication of what has evolved between us. Our agreement has served to preserve the spell of our sexual attraction, while allowing us to avoid deciphering any deeper meaning.

"Hey," I say, wrapping my arms around his wide shoulders. He smells of sandalwood and vanilla. It's so hard not to brush my fingers through his hair, down his face to his lips. I shove my hands into my pockets.

He surveys the rec center's buzz. "Put me to work."

"Really? I mean, I just wanted to invite you as, you know, like my date."

"I know, *babe*. But from what I just heard, there's plenty of work that needs to be done." My heart swells with desire for this man, this billionaire space entrepreneur who's willing to roll up his sleeves and pitch in for a small town fundraiser.

"If you insist," I say, digging into the grocery bag I've brought. "Here's a stack of paper table clothes. Can you open these and put them out?"

"I can and I will. But tablecloths? Give me something meaty!"

"Mmm, insubordinate, huh?" I quip. "Start there and we'll see."

As I hear the snap of his flapping open the first tablecloth, I grab an apron from my bag, secure its canvas ties around my back and head into the kitchen to check on the food prep.

The music has shifted from Kanye to Taylor. A woman pulls bread from the large industrial oven. The smell of roasted garlic and butter makes me realize how hungry I am. A man stirs green beans in an enormous copper pot. Two women are chopping carrots for salad, and another is mixing dough for chocolate chip cookies.

I feel an arm around my shoulder and turn around to see Noah. He's wearing navy pants and a dark green crew neck sweater.

"Oh, hey," I say, "thanks for coming early."

"Madeline's a friend of a friend. Happy to help. What can I do?"

I place my hands on my hips and continue my survey of the kitchen, my eyes landing on a plastic bowl. "Looks like you and I should start dicing these tomatoes."

"Let's do it," he says, clapping his hands.

We stand side by side at the large metal island at the center of the kitchen, dicing beefsteak tomatoes with long serrated knives, our fingers quickly sticky with the sweet juice. Noah tells me a delicious rumor about one of our colleagues at the tourism board who apparently hooked up with a visitor who'd come in with questions about local hikes and turned out to also be our boss's niece. I laugh and am reminded of our easy chemistry, one so apparent that our HR rep once asked — for "due diligence" purposes — if we were dating.

A flash of pink appears in the doorway and I see Ren standing there observing us. He gives me a half smile that's hard to read.

"Tablecloths on," he says. "Hey man," he says to Noah.

"'Sup," Noah replies.

I tilt the bowl of tomatoes toward me and see that we've already gotten through most of them. "Noah, can you take it from here?"

"Yeah, sure," he says.

I lead Ren back out into the main hall. "You're promoted from tablecloths to silent auction. Let's set up these bidding sheets and items."

In true Lake Lyla fashion, there are generous donations from local businesses including a year's supply of free lattes from Bernie's, a gift certificate from The Book Mark, two nights at the Inn and a ski pass for the upcoming season at Bigrock Mountain.

As soon as the silent auction table is ready, a delivery arrives from Leaves & Petals, the garden center where Summer worked for many years, which has donated centerpieces for the tables, a lovely combination of mums and pansies in cute jars, all of which will be available to guests who buy lottery tickets.

"What next?" Ren says once we've placed the centerpieces.

I check the time on my phone. "Probably should begin manning the ticket table outside."

I'm delighted to see there are already people lining up to purchase tickets to support Madeline. The ticket table is under the building's awning but it doesn't shield us from the wind gusts and mist. By the time everyone is checked in 30 minutes later, my hair is damp. We head inside and join the volunteers who are passing out heaping plates of spaghetti to the diners.

A local high school band plays smooth jazz during dinner. Once everyone is served, we sit with Greta, Summer, Cole and Winter, and I feel an odd pang. I try not to think about what will happen after this night, after our final agreed-upon date.

But facts are facts. There were *reasons* for Operation Voltaire. Ren's desire to remain single, a status that has served him, that he's comfortable with, that enables him to focus on his work. My commitment — my *promise* to myself — to understand who I am, my commitment to not mindlessly taking the same path, to partnering up yet again.

No matter how sexy Ren is, no matter how good the *sex* with Ren is, I must respect him — and myself — and accept the past weeks for what they were: a mythical interlude, a temporary distraction formed by mutual agreement,

As cookies are served after spaghetti, a few people speak, including a doctor who explains Madeline's condition and how effective the medication is, and Madeline's parents who tearfully thank the Lake Lyla community for its support. The jazz band resumes playing as everyone is encouraged to mingle and squeeze in final bids in the silent auction.

Ren roams the auction tables while I check on kitchen cleanup. A half hour later the hall begins to empty. It's now fully raining outside, transforming the evening into a cozy, fall night.

We gather the sheets from the silent auction to the noisy clanks of metal chairs and tables being dismantled and stacked. Every auction item received at least a few bids and a quick glance shows that we've likely exceeded our fundraising goal. I pick up the last bid sheet, the one that doesn't have any item attached to it but instead is just a straight donation sheet. Amidst the pledges for $20, $50 and $100, I spot an addition donation of $25,000.

"Holy shit," I say, drawing my finger across the line to find the donor's name. Perhaps it's the owner of the Inn or one of Madeline's relatives who traveled to the fundraiser from Southern California.

Edward Lewis.

I march over to Ren, who's helping Madeline's father stack chairs in the corner. I pull him aside. "Is...is this you?"

He shrugs, but his eyes twinkle.

I'm so touched that my rib cage feels too small, unable to contain my ballooning heart. In this moment, Ren's being a billionaire doesn't seem gross or abhorrent, but simply enchanting.

Chapter 21

REN

Bernie's hasn't changed much since the first time I set foot here a couple of months ago. There's still a fire roaring in the corner. Bernadette is still behind the counter, even at this late hour. But now a felt bucket in the shape of a bright orange Halloween pumpkin rests on the counter, filled with bite-sized candy bars.

Autumn and I just left the spaghetti feed fundraiser. We've come here to Bernie's, as we pledged at the start, to formally, officially conclude our contract since this is where Operation Voltaire was devised.

Next to the Halloween candy is a miniature, leafless tree with construction paper leaves attached with yarn to the skinny stick branches.

"What's this?" I ask.

"Our gratitude tree," Bernadette says, proudly. "Just put it out this morning. Here's a leaf for each of you. Write what you're grateful for and we'll hang it alongside the others."

I look over at Autumn. Maybe I'm imagining it but, like me, she has an aura of anticipatory melancholy, despite the runaway success of tonight's spaghetti fundraiser. Thanks in large part to Autumn, Madeline now has enough funds to purchase at least a couple of years' worth of her life-saving medicine. Meanwhile, Autumn and I are at an unanticipated crossroads, yet I'm pretty sure neither of us knows what side of the divide we'll land on. I surely don't.

I like Autumn. I really, really like her. And it's precisely because I care about her that I want her to finally have what *she* desperately wants — independence. Even though, by definition, that means I'll no longer be part of her life.

"While you're writing those, what can I get you?" Bernadette says.

"A big mug of apple cinnamon tea for me," Autumn says.

I study the menu on the wall behind the counter and then eye the pastries remaining in the glass case.

"You like pumpkin?" Bernadette says.

"Like pumpkin spice lattes?" I wrinkle my nose. "Sorry, I know it's like unconstitutional or something, but no."

Bernadette points to a pie dish in the case with one slice left. "Homemade pumpkin pie. Crust has the perfect texture — toothy but flaky. Don't mean to brag, but it's pretty freakin' awesome."

"Jeez, pumpkin pie...it really is that time of year," I say. Time has flown in the last several weeks. "Sold. And I'll have the same tea as Autumn."

Bernadette begins preparing our order and we finger the paper leaves. Autumn uncaps her pen, leans over the counter and begins to write. I follow suit.

What am I grateful for?

Autumn being by my side at the Infinity Symposium, enabling me to focus on my keynote address, which received a buzz-worthy response that exceeded my expectations. Her companionship at the conferences also enabled me to make business connections without being distracted by offers of romantic set-ups. Her being there also centered me, showed me the upside of having a partner, a companion. It was a glimpse into what life would be like not being alone.

I'm grateful for mind-blowing sex. But I can't write that.

I'm grateful for Autumn being a potent reminder of something I learned long ago at camp. She reminded me of tikun olam, of using personal action to repair the world, whether through a spaghetti feed for somebody who needs financial support during an illness or simply a scarf on a cold day.

I'm grateful that Operation Voltaire allowed me to meet Autumn's family. Being at that wedding changed me — I'm still feeling the effects. I got to see first-hand a different kind of family from my own, and I've come to appreciate a wholly different kind of abundance than what my parents and I focused on.

I know what to write on my leaf.

Autumn finishes writing at the same time as I do and clutches her leaf to her chest. "Wanna share?"

I nod.

She turns her leaf around. Behind the lenses of her glasses, her eyes glisten. In block letters, she's written: "Tikun olam."

I flip my paper around to show her my own two words: "Lake Lyla."

Her lips curl and she grabs her lower lip with her teeth. Then she opens her mouth and I wait eagerly for her response. But just then Bernadette slides our teas and my pie across the counter. Wordlessly, we grab them and make our way to the back of the cafe to "our" table, the one where we first hammered out the precise details of our contract. The crackling fire creates a thick, smoky, almost haunted atmosphere for this, our final meeting.

"We did pretty good, huh?" Autumn says.

I tilt my head in question.

She lifts a shoulder tentatively, a half-hearted shrug. "You know, we accomplished what we set out to do. Your conference...it seemed really successful."

There's a question in her tone so I nod vigorously. "Yes. Yes. Very successful. Your being there allowed me to maximize what was important."

She nods more definitively, businesslike now. "Good, good. And for me, going through life cycle events as a triplet, it's...it's weird. We're always compared. Summer found the love of her life so now everyone asks when that'll happen for me, for Winter. Having you as a date at the wedding, it took the pressure off. I'm glad Greta convinced me to bring a date after all."

I'm reminded that like me with Leah, none of this was her idea.

"And then you coming tonight, helping with the event, making our relationship seem less like a one-off.... Not to mention, your donation. Unbelievable." She does that adorable thing where she takes a tiny finger and glides hair behind her ear.

"Operation Voltaire will go down in the annals of fake dating as a resounding success," I say.

"Like Edward and Vivian, I guess we're both just good...actors."

A piercing stab hits me in the sternum. I clear my throat to get it to go away.

She blows on her tea and takes a sip. "What's next for you?"

So this is really it.

I take a bite of pie to divert my attention from the knifelike jolts in my torso. "Next? Um, got a meeting in New York City in a few days. Then I'll be turning to capitalizing" – I'm starting to hate that word – "on more of the connections I made at the conference. So, basically, more of the same."

"Status quo."

Her words make me long to return with her to the presidential suite, to feel her soft curves beneath me, to inhale the smell of her. Because, Jesus, that was anything but the status quo.

But we're here to terminate a contract, to dissolve it. The sex...we clearly just got carried away. Was it really just proximity? Hormones? I simply can't presume anything more. Because even if I wanted to continue it, to expand it, to explore it, Autumn is committed to living on her own for once — it was the whole reason for Operation Voltaire in the first place. And because I care about her, I respect her goal, even though the thought of us returning to our previous lives hurts. It hurts far more than I ever would have expected when Leah first tossed Autumn's profile onto my desk back in September. It feels like a lifetime ago.

I cough. "And you? What's next?"

She glances down, her hands wrapped around the large white mug. Her eyelashes are impossibly long. She raises her gaze and looks back up at me. I want to draw a finger along her cheekbone, to trace her eyebrows with my lips.

"Ski season. It's huge here. We get thousands of visitors and there are all kinds of events, including the Snow Spectacle and several holiday celebrations at the Inn. So, basically, busy at work."

"Anything else? Animals to rescue, right? Funds to be raised?"

She brings a finger to the bridge of her glasses, pushing them up. "Always."

"You're a good person, Autumn Sky."

She's quiet for a moment, and her stare feels as if it's penetrating my spirit. "You too, Ren. You really are."

Something unspoken hovers in the air. I feel that she wants to say more, but maybe it's just hope on my part. Still, I lean forward and look squarely into her eyes.

Bernadette approaches, breaking the spell. "How's the pie?"

I exhale. "Delicious."

"Knew you'd like it." She scoops up the dish and swipes up the crumbs with a towel. "Drink up because we're closing in ten minutes."

Autumn nods and Bernadette heads to the kitchen.

"Almost forgot!" Autumn says, reaching around to the canvas bag hanging on the back of her chair. She pulls out a rolled up piece of paper tied with a dark green bow. "A little thank you for, you know, holding up your end of the bargain."

Shit.

I didn't even think of getting her a gift. Either way, all I really have to give is...money. And she's not Vivian, the Pretty Woman hooker.

But then I hear my grandmother's voice, as I often do in times like these. "All you must do is be gracious, Ren," she'd say. "Thank her genuinely and properly for the gift, even if you're embarrassed for not having one to give in return."

I gently slide the ribbon off the tube. Then I slowly unroll the paper. It's thicker than computer paper, thinner than the construction paper gratitude leaves. What's gradually revealed is a stunning, hand-drawn map of Lake Lyla.

"I know your cartography collection is a lot fancier than this. But I made this for you so, you know, you'll remember."

Chapter 22

AUTUMN

Bernadette props the front door open as she lugs the large sandwich board sign with today's specials back inside. The air whooshing in is heavy and damp with that distinctive, storm's-a-brewing smell. I shiver, the chill reaching my bones despite the hot tea. Back inside, Bernadette lowers the blinds, and the cafe now mimics the dark that's been descending earlier and earlier in recent weeks.

A little more than a month ago, I was appalled that Greta had signed me up on Billionaire Rendezvous without my knowledge. I never would have imagined the extreme feelings that would result — the unsuspected, electrifying delight in being with Ren, and my gloominess about the imminent, abrupt conclusion to Operation Voltaire.

When you live in a small town, the place you've lived most of your life, you get complacent, sure that you know everything to expect, certain that life has few surprises in store. In truth, that's part of the *joy* of this kind of life. Living here, on a lake in a small Northern California mountain town, is predictable. So when somebody new arrives and shakes things up, it's as unsettling as it is delightful.

Did I expect to develop feelings for the man who accompanied me to my sister's wedding by contract?

Did I expect to actually fall for a billionaire and all his showy displays of wealth?

Did I expect to be drawn to a man who loves wine and maps, who purchased his own jet because he's grossed out by germs?

A man who willingly listens to me pluck awkwardly on a beat-up guitar?

A man who's obsessed with space?

A man whose touch — equal parts gentle and rough — turns me inside out?

Operation Voltaire first required that I *act* as if I liked him. And now, it's come to this: I have to *act* like the contract terminating is not slicing my heart open.

Ren is a visionary. He's ambitious. And it's because I care about him that I must resume my normal life here without him. I will not distract him from his life goals the way other women have long tried to do.

Not to mention the fact that before this temporary interlude, I'd committed to getting to know myself. They call the twenties the defining decade. For the first seven years of my twenties, it hasn't been true for me. It's time I define who Autumn is.

If I don't understand soon who I am, I fear it'll be too late and I'll forever be simply the middle triplet, simply Winter's identical sister.

So I must accept that the magic I've experienced with Ren is fleeting. Living with the emptiness I've already begun to feel whenever Ren has returned to San Francisco in the last months is the first, most critical step in me finally becoming an individual.

"Okay, kids," Bernadette says, "closing time!"

178

My choice is to stand, that first step in moving forward, or collapse in a heap. With great effort, I rise, throwing my canvas bag over my shoulder. A fiery stone settles deep in my belly.

With a gentleness that's almost painful to watch, Ren rerolls the map I drew for him and slowly slides it in the inside pocket of his cashmere coat. I had fun drawing the map, making sure to include our shared landmarks: Bernie's, the Inn, The Book Mark, the dock where Summer and Cole got married, the Noble Peasant, where we shared our first kiss. And in the corner there's a picture-in-picture portion of the map that shows Lake Lyla nestled at the northeastern tip of California in relation to both San Francisco and Seattle.

As we pass the counter on our way out, Bernadette hands Ren a brown paper bag with a few muffins that weren't sold today but will still be delicious tomorrow morning. I press my lips together realizing that Ren will eat them back home in San Francisco. He's departing in minutes.

The yowling wind and the hum of a jet engine a mile in the sky above accompany us as we walk to our cars. When we're on the next block, a group exits a bar laughing raucously, an acute contrast to the somber mood floating between me and Ren.

One of the guys in the group notices me, and his face changes in recognition.

"Oh, hey, Winter! How's it going?" he says breezily as he and his friends walk past us.

"Fine, thanks," I murmur.

Ren halts and looks over at me, his eyes wide.

"Sometimes," I shrug, "it's just easier to pretend."

Chapter 23

AUTUMN

I have to get out of my apartment.

I've spent all day in my pajamas. Outside my window, the sky is colorless, not quite white, not quite grey. I've picked up every book on my nightstand but none keeps my attention for more than a paragraph. I start to binge everything from Gossip Girl to Friends to the Amazing Race but it's all a bore and I turn each show off after just a few scenes.

I go cross-eyed staring into space.

In the mid-afternoon, my phone rings. It's Winter.

"What's wrong?" she asks before I've even completed my "hello."

I don't bother asking how she knows because I know how she knows. It's the same reason I knew she was coming down with mono when we were in college even though we went to schools three hundred miles apart. It's the reason I once woke with an unexplained bruise on my finger only to learn that Winter had cut herself in the same exact place the night before. We're not twins but we're identical. It just...happens.

I sigh. "Just got the blahs, I guess."

"Have you made your favorite tea?"

I lift my mug as if she can see it, though we're audio only. "Got a mug right here."

"Gossip Girl?"

"Not cutting it today."

"Friends?"

"Also, nope."

"Man," she says. "Bring out the big guns? Want me to come over and we can watch Pretty Woman? I'll make my famous coconut oil popcorn."

"NO!" I say, too sharply I realize as soon as it's out of my mouth.

"Jeez, okay."

"Sorry, just a little testy."

"Tell me why you two broke up."

Little does Winter know that Ren and I weren't actually dating at all, that we spent so much time together because of a formal agreement. "I just...can we not right now, Win?"

I don't want to reveal the true nature of my "relationship" with Ren, and I don't want to have to explain why I made the agreement in the first place, why I promised myself I wouldn't jump into yet another relationship without first spending time on my own learning, finally, who I am. I also don't want to confess how badly I want to break that promise, to call Ren and tell him how much I miss our conversations, how desperately I want to get naked with him.

Not breaking the promise to myself is breaking *me*.

By denying myself a connection unlike any I've ever felt before and probably won't ever feel again, am I cutting off my nose to spite my face?

But it's not just about me. It never is. There are always two of us. And now I care too much about Ren to try to convince him that we have to be together when he, too, voiced explicit reasons for wanting something artificial, something temporary.

At the same time, making up a story, a lie about why we "broke up" feels oddly disloyal too.

"I just don't have it in me right now," I say, with a pang, finishing the thought out loud.

Winter exhales. "Okay, I hear you. And I'm here for you whenever you need."

"I know."

"One final suggestion...."

Despite how awful I feel, I can't help but smile. My womb mate is pushy, but she does it out of love. "Okay."

"Get out of the house."

I groan. It's cold outside. I'm comfortable in the sweats I slept in.

"I can see you in my mind's eye. You're on the couch."

Right.

"You've been eyeing your guitar all day, one side of your brain telling you to pick it up and play, the other side saying it's all just too much effort."

Right again.

"You haven't brushed your teeth. You stink a little. The thought of even wetting a washcloth for a hooker bath makes you want to cry." I'm grateful Winter stops there. She could have gone deeper, reminding me of rough breakups that made me do things I'm not proud of — calling one old boyfriend so many times he got a new phone number, almost losing my job because I broke into sobs whenever a Lake Lyla visitor asked about a particular beach that held special memories with another boyfriend I'd recently broken up with.

"I know this not because I'm your sister, Aut. I know this because you're clearly heartbroken. I've been there too. We've all been there. I will say, though, that you seem more distraught about Ren than any man ever. So there's that. But, anyway, get out of the house."

A golf ball forms in my throat, hearing Ren's name out loud. I can't respond.

"Autie," she says, her voice softening. "Is Greta working today?"

"Uh huh," I sputter. If I say anything else, the sobs will flow.

"Go. Now. See dogs and cats. Fill yourself with some best friend energy."

I think of Zippers, his crooked teeth and splotches of white amidst the black and brown on his four-pound body. Greta's pet grooming place *does* have an overpowering scent of lavender shampoo so she won't even know if I stink. I don't even have to do the hooker bath.

"Okay," I whisper. "Thanks, Win."

"What are sisters for?"

I stand even before ending the call so that momentum for getting out of the house begins. Twenty minutes later, I enter Tip Top Tails. Greta's got some kind of Doodle mix on the table and she's peering through magnifying glasses as she precisely trims around the dog's mouth.

"The last person who groomed this big guy made him look like my eighty-five-year-old grandfather. He's not even *two*. I'm bringing the puppy back!" she says without looking up at me.

From a tiny dog bed in the corner, Zippers spots me and darts over, standing on his hind legs and whimpering for me to pick him up, which I do. His fur has softened under Greta's care, now that he's on a proper diet and no longer scrounging for scraps on the street.

"Still no luck finding this little nugget a home?" I ask, rubbing my nose against Zippers's.

"No," Greta says, squatting to check the Doodle's face at eye level. "I'm telling you, he's not interested in most people. One woman showed promise but when she brought her existing dog in to meet him, it was not a love match. Those are few and far between."

I start to cry.

Greta puts down her shears. "Oh, Aut, I'm sorry you're hurting."

I bite my upper lip and snuggle Zippers closer. "It's okay."

"It's not okay," she says, putting an arm around my shoulder and leading me to the chair she has for clients who arrive early for pick-up. She kneels down before me. We both pet Zippers. "I feel responsible for your pain. I'm the one who found Ren on that site, I'm the one who convinced you to meet him. And worst of all, I *knew* you'd fall in love."

"What?" I wipe my nose on the sleeve of my Habitat for Humanity sweatshirt. "How could you possibly know that?"

"*Because*." She grabs a tissue from the nearby table covered in bottles, combs, clippers and towels. "You're Taurus and he's a Virgo. When those two earth signs collide, hedonism is downright unavoidable."

The pursuit of pleasure was not *our problem.*

"But it's more than that," she adds. "You're four signs apart. It's called a Trine. And it triggers a special kind of harmony, a sort of unspoken kinship. The Zodiac system would say that you two should have felt...understood by one another. At a core level. Like without having to explain yourself. It's like feeling at home. And I looked at your moon signs, your rising sign, your lunar nodes, the position of your planets in the twelfth house...all of it pointed to one of the most intense, compatible, enriching matches I've ever seen." She dabs my cheeks with the tissue. "I still can't figure out why it didn't last."

The man is rough as he helps me into my harness. It's nothing like the tender – but still hungry – way that Ren undressed me those times in his suite at the Inn. The man's unruly beard distracts me at least, not only from memories of Ren, but also from what I'm about to do. I look at Greta, who's also getting strapped in.

"Remind me again why we're doing this?" I ask.

"Because it's supposed to be fun. And by my assessment, you need a little perking up."

It's a couple of days after I visited Greta at work. This afternoon we're at Tangled Up, a ropes course on south shore that, after today, will be closed for winter until April. From afar, the clear sky may fool one into thinking it's spring here at Lake Lyla, but the temperatures are hovering just over 40 degrees and a mixture of rain and snow are predicted in the next two weeks.

According to Tangled Up's brochure, the ropes course promises to be an "exhilarating romp designed to challenge limits." I really hope so, because Greta is right, I need perking up. It's been a week since Ren left Lake Lyla for San Francisco. Per the terms of our agreement, we haven't communicated since. Despite my commitment to singlehood, the last week has left me distracted and irritable. I even snapped at a tourism board caller — telling him that if he wanted to find a pick-up lacrosse game, he'd have to call the tourism board for *bougie-ville* — and my boss instructed me to head home for the remainder of the day.

Zippers, who's come with us, brings his tiny front paws onto my calf, his tail wagging. I lift him up and snuggle him in my arms as the ropes course guy clips the harness around my back.

"He never does that with me," Greta says of Zippers. "Even though I'm the one who feeds him, shaved off all his matts. He's still kind of aloof. Can't figure out why he likes you."

"Gee, thanks," I say, squeezing Zippers before placing him back on the ground.

"Good to go," the bearded guy says and gives us instructions for maneuvering through the rope swings, wobbly bridges, swinging logs, tightropes, cargo nets and horizontal climbing walls.

"And the dog can hang out here?" Greta says as we snap on our helmets. "His leash tied up to that pole?"

"No problem," the guy says. "Dogs wait in that spot all the time."

After a too-brief lesson in using the two carabiners, one after the other, to safely travel up a plank and over to the first ladder, we take our first steps on the course. Initially, we're not too far off the ground and the carabiner clips are close together. But then, by design, the plank we're walking gets steeper and the clips farther apart. The path leads us to a huge tree with metal plates hammered into the trunk. It's then that the course becomes slightly terrifying. My brain knows that I'm strapped in, that if I fall, I will be caught before hitting the ground. But my central nervous system doesn't get it, only sensing the air around me as I climb up the tree ladder.

I'll give it to Greta. This activity requires hyper focus, which helps take my mind off of Ren.

We're quiet as we make our way up the tree to the first wooden platform about 100 feet up. The platform wiggles with our dual weight.

"Whoa," Greta says, clutching the trunk as I move from crawling to standing. "Feels like an earthquake."

In between pants, I shiver.

"Should we, uh, sit for a minute?" Greta proposes, her voice as shaky as the wooden platform.

"Just a reminder this was *your* idea."

The view is worth the discomfort of being so high up. This south shore vantage point of the lake is different from our normal north shore location. From here, I can view the mountains I'm normally directly beside. I'm reminded of their majesty, their sturdiness. Below and to the right, we see Beaver Moon Vineyards, which owns this ropes course and where we're headed after we return to solid ground. The vines are tidy and neat and their symmetry settles my nerves.

"How you doing, Autie?"

I shrug.

"I feel badly."

"For what? I agreed to come here."

"No, about Ren. Setting you up with him for Sum's wedding – I started it. I had no idea that you two would fall so quickly, so hard for each other. Or that it would end so abruptly. I mean, is there a reason you two can't *actually* date?"

"Um, remember why I needed a fake date to Summer's wedding in the first place? I made a commitment to myself, to not be connected to somebody, whether it's Winter or yet one more boyfriend."

"I know, I know. 'Individuation.'"

When I hear it out loud, it strikes me that individuation – just like triangulation – also sounds like strangulation.

All the more reason to see my commitment through.

I *need* to feel this loneliness. I must prove to myself that being alone is okay. I must discover what I'm all about when I don't have a partner.

"What about Ren, though? He's in love with you."

I snap my head to look at her. "In *love* with me? The altitude up here is affecting your oxygen levels."

She skews her eyebrows. "C'mon, Autie. Anyone who got within three feet of you two could see how he feels about you...."

My heart hurts. I shake my head to correct her. "Ren is as committed to his company, his vision, his professional goals as I am to discovering myself. Plus, he's an only child long used to being on his own. He prefers it. As much as being part of a trio or a pair is my comfort zone, his being solo is how *he's* comfortable. So, anyway, we were never a real thing."

"It's okay to miss him," she says and then grabs hold of the tree trunk and slowly lifts herself to standing. With every movement, the platform shakes and wobbles.

She lowers a hand and I take it. She pulls me up to standing. Dozens of feet below, Zippers barks and turns circles in excitement as he spots us. I give him a little wave.

We continue through the course, first walking sideways along thick ropes, our toes curling like bird talons on a perch, our hands sliding across thick wires overhead. We cross over to two more wooden platforms, each higher than the previous. With each tremble and shake of the wood beneath us, we squeal and shriek like we did as kids sledding down the hill behind Greta's house.

The final platform is 150 feet high and the views are striking. Even the Inn's palatial whiteness nestled into the mountain just above Rowan Beach is visible. We pause, taking in our hometown from afar, finches and sparrows floating and chirping around us.

The course finale is a long zipline ride that squeakily delivers us to the starting point. While newly invigorated, I'm still sad, unable to stop myself from wondering what Ren is doing in this moment.

The bearded guy helps us out of the harnesses. I scoop Zippers up and we meander down a path to Beaver Moon, the neighboring winery.

As we walk, it feels odd to have my feet back on the earth. It's like when we were kids and we'd spend an hour roller skating at the rink for a birthday party. When it was time for cake, walking into the dining area in sneakers felt bizarre, like steadiness was foreign.

"I noted on our reservation that you don't drink," Greta says as we approach the winery. "They're known for their food too and I just thought you'd enjoy learning the history of the vineyard."

"Thanks. At work, I often get questions about this place so it's good for me to finally check it out."

At the end of the path connecting Tangled Up to Beaver Moon, we're greeted by a hostess at a stunning outdoor kitchen, complete with fire pits, tables, couches and outdoor chandeliers underneath a thick canopy. We're guided to a table where a plate of cheeses and several small bowls of grapes await. Wine samples for Greta and sparkling water for me have already been poured.

"Our lake level soil is unlike soil anywhere else in the world," our waitress explains. "This merlot here is unusually dark and dry, with hints of cooked raspberry."

"Delicious," Greta says after her first sip.

"This is a sample of the grape it's made with," the waitress says to me.

I taste it. The purple skin is tough and the fruit is unusually bitter.

"Now this one," she continues, "is fresh and fruity, expertly balanced with a pleasing mouth feel."

It's a struggle not to roll my eyes. Even if I did drink, I doubt I'd grasp the nuances of the varietals. The whole thing is kind of snobby, I think, then chide myself for being a grump. Greta's loving every sip and I can't help but think how much Ren would enjoy it here too.

When the waitress leaves to retrieve new bottles to sample, Greta gets up from the table. "Lots of tiny sips are already catching up with me. Gotta pee!"

I take a skinny breadstick from the jelly jar at the center of the table and take a bite.

"Autumn!"

I turn around to see Noah.

"I'm not following you! I swear," he says affably. "Family here from out of town." He points to four people being seated at a nearby table. "Been here before?"

I shake my head. "A friend brought me. I'm not into wine but I figured it'd be helpful for work for me to finally see this place for myself."

"Ever been to the adventure course next door?"

"As of about thirty minutes ago, yes."

"Hey," he says, scratching the back of his neck and glancing over at his relatives, who are already tasting their first wines. "I've been meaning to ask you something. Since we always seem to be at the same places outside of work — synagogue, The Book Mark, here...." He clears his throat. "And I always enjoy our conversations. I'm wondering if you ever want to, like, you know, go out to dinner or a movie or something?"

Shit.

I had a feeling this might happen. And it's not that I hadn't thought about it myself. Noah is handsome and funny and smart. So much so that before Greta surreptitiously signed me up for Billionaire Rendezvous I came *this* close to asking *him* to Summer's wedding. He's like a replica of many of my past boyfriends but, I realize now, without that essential zing or spark.

Maybe if I'd never been with Ren, I might have taken a chance to see if a spark might develop over time. But now that I've experienced that special kind of electricity with Ren...I just can't. Plus, *no dating right now.*

I hesitate a moment too long before replying and the turned-down corners of Noah's mouth and his deep exhale show that he's already gauged my answer. He lowers his chin and nods in defeat. "That man I've seen you with...at the bookstore, at the spaghetti fundraiser. Is he your boyfriend?"

"We just broke up," I say, hoping the catch in my voice isn't noticeable. "I just don't think it's a good idea...I mean, I have a policy not to date at work."

It's the easiest, kindest, most reasonable response. No need to go into the whole *no dating right now* thing.

He presses his lips together and nods. "Had a feeling you might say that."

"It's nothing personal —"

"No, no, I get it," he says, then smiles.

God, he really is cute.

He continues. "I didn't just blow our friendship, did I? I don't want anything to be weird. I mean, who else will I gossip with about annoying visitors? About the latest episode of the Amazing Race?"

"Not weird at all, Noah. Swear."

Just then, Greta returns. "What'd I miss?"

"Greta, this is Noah. We work together."

They shake hands cordially and then Noah heads over to join his family.

"Wow," she whispers. "*He's* cute."

Chapter 24

REN

Raindrops splatter on the thick plastic oval windows as we begin our descent. Leah and I are returning to the Bay Area after a few days in New York City for meetings with an NYU astrophysicist and the CEO of a biotech company focused on developing supplements to help human bodies adapt quickly to space travel. Looking out the window, down at the Rockies, then the Sierras, I feel as if I'm straddling, hovering between places, between time. Here in my private plane, with home-brewed kombucha and plush blankets at the ready, there's still a sense of unsteadiness akin to my childhood, a childhood without nightly dinners with my parents, without siblings to center me. Leah, my anchor, is next to me. With the plane's Wi-Fi available for only a few more minutes, I exchange texts with my grandmother, who fills me in on her latest mah jongg tournament and sends me photos from Sukkot, the Jewish harvest festival, which she celebrated last month with friends. My grandmother's social life has always outpaced my own.

Then I pull up my own social media feed, the one I share with only my most trustworthy friends. I stare wistfully at my last post, the one of me and Autumn from Summer's wedding. We're cheek-to-cheek, pupils dilated. A lock of her hair is flying across my chin in the wind. Our teeth are on full display from our wide smiles. We look like teenagers.

Why am I torturing myself?

I'm about to close the app with cinematic ferocity when I notice I've got a DM. I click the icon and see it's from Kenny, who forwarded me the latest post from that stupid Courting Castillo account.

It's a photo of me and Autumn from the first night of the Infinity Symposium. That deep red gown shows off all her curves. We're gazing at each other like we have a wicked secret.

The headline reads, "Girls Just Want to Have Funds."

I scan the first few comments, which range from, "She's stunning!" to "A man is not a financial plan" to "That's a wallet lightener if I've ever seen one."

Shit.

I'm not a scientist but in school I was always far more drawn to science than the humanities. I mean, Moby Dick can fuck off out of my English syllabus. Give me the scientific method any day. Hypothesis, prediction, testing, experiments, analysis — a time-tested, sure-fire way to prove or disprove an idea.

Over the years, I've thought about the scientific method in relation to romance, to relationships. In my twenties, I tried different kinds of relationships, testing them like a researcher — getting set up by friends, dating women in my field, going out with women who had common interests, asking out women who were wildly different from me. Each test failed — no relationship stuck.

And I should have remembered all of that.

With Autumn, it felt different. I felt that she liked me not because of my money but in spite of it. With Autumn, I felt more myself than even when I'm alone. I could let my guard down with her. I even revealed to her the real reason I bought my own plane, my obsession with sanitizing. The only other person in my life who knows those things is Leah.

But in the end, the very reasons we came together for Operation Voltaire turned out to be the exact hurdles our "relationship" couldn't overcome — no matter how easy our conversations, no matter how hot the sex, no matter how joyful I felt just being near her. The experiment, such as it was, failed. Those feelings of attraction, of connection could most likely be explained by run-of-the-mill biology: electrical impulses in the brain, simple hormonal activity. I shouldn't have let myself *feel* that much, to even *speculate* whether we could really be together. I should have remembered that no matter how good it felt or how desperately I wanted it, I'm just not meant for that kind of love.

Without even speaking to my grandmother directly, I know she'd insist I stop "should-ing" all over myself. It's one of her favorite sayings and something she lives by. "Trust yourself," she always insists. "Trust the Universe."

I instruct myself to remember my grandmother's entreaty. I need to fill up my brain, to push out the torrent of thoughts of Autumn, my hope that she hasn't seen this goddamn Courting Castillo post. To that end, I pull up on my iPad a 60-page proposal from an electric spacecraft propulsion company that needs review.

A few minutes later, at the flight attendant's instruction, I shut off my devices and look around. I see the aircraft's clean opulence in a new way now. I still like that it's mine and mine alone and enables me to travel whenever I need and I can do so knowing that this seat hasn't been used by thousands of others. I tell myself I'm not an elitist, just a germaphobe. But since meeting Autumn, I've begun to question whether this massive convenience is a just and responsible use of money.

The pilot glides us into a gentle landing at a small, private airport north of San Francisco. Leah and I walk through the airport lounge, its granite tables and artisan coffee assaulting me with its grandiosity. Just outside the lounge, Matthew is waiting. He takes our carry-ons, one in each hand, and rolls them to the van. Leah and I respond to our never-ending messages as we drive into the city.

It's still very early morning in California. We left New York at daybreak and napped on the plane. Fewer than 40 minutes after touching down, we're already back in the office, which strikes me as sterile, almost soulless, but for my map of Argentina, the home of my ancestors. This new discomfort in an old setting jars me.

We settle at the big table to review the week's upcoming calendar, complete with another conference, this one in Illinois, and video meetings with no fewer than seven companies with promising investment potential. Though the door is open, the receptionist knocks on the door frame before entering with two items: a pink bakery box and a cardboard tube. Leah takes the pink box. I take the tube.

"What do you have there?" I ask, as I struggle to pry off the tube's tight plastic top.

"Beignets."

"From *New Orleans*?"

"Yep," she says. "Had them flown in."

I went to Tulane University and still crave the powdered sugar-covered dough bombs, especially during times of stress.

For the first time in years I wonder how much an extravagance like shipping fresh pastries costs and consider whether all those resources could have been better used. "Why?"

"Because you're a wreck, Ren. You barely asked any questions during our meeting at NYU and you've been grumpy and withdrawn and I figured you could use a boost."

I peer into the box, which smells of yeast and has patches of dark brown on the bottom where grease has pooled on the cardboard. I take one. "Appreciated, but unnecessary."

"I disagree. I had to bring out the big guns. I haven't seen you this...distracted...in...I don't know when. Maybe eighth grade? When your parents were late to our middle school graduation?"

I take a bite. "You're a good friend."

The beignet tastes not quite how it normally does and I'm not sure if it's because of the delay from having it shipped or because it feels as if *everything* has changed in the last week, since I last saw Autumn. In New York, a city I normally love, the fall colors of Central Park struck me as muted, less vibrant. The world-class symphony at Lincoln Center sounded tinny and dissonant and made me long to hear Autumn strumming '70s folk on her crummy guitar.

I finish the beignet and finally wrestle the round plastic lid off the cardboard tube, creating a popping sound. I tap the open end onto the glass table and a rolled, plastic-encased map slides out. I wipe my hands on a napkin, squirt hand sanitizer from the dispenser on the table, and rub my palms together.

"New addition to your collection?"

"Yup," I say, though this particular purchase is actually of little value in the cartography world. I tear off the plastic and slowly unfurl the map, which sounds like the turning of aged newspaper pages.

"Looks old," Leah says, standing to peer over it. "Is that Tahoe?"

I shake my head. "Lake Lyla. From the early twentieth century."

It's old enough that there's no designation of businesses like the Inn or Bernie's or The Book Mark. Instead, the pinkish illustration highlights railroad lines and tributaries, mountains and public beaches and parks. On the lower right, there's a description, written in fountain pen, of the town: "Settled by Lyla Lansberg. Immigrant, leader, organizer."

Autumn's great-great-great grandmother. I believe Autumn takes after her, despite the many generations separating them.

"Quite beautiful," Leah says. "You planning to show it to Autumn?"

I shake my head. "That's over."

"Why, Ren?"

I reroll the map. "You should know better than anyone, Leah. In fact, you're the only one who knows why. My time with Autumn...it was a contract, an act."

"Was it now?" Her stare, probing and acute, reminds me that there are pros and cons to decades-old friendships. I can't get anything past my best friend.

"I've got a business to run," I say.

"What's that got to do with anything?"

"It's got everything to do with everything. I needed a pre-tend date so I could focus at the Infinity Symposium."

"That was *one* event. One event when you needed to stave off the normal fortune hunters. But there's nothing that says you can't have a *real* relationship."

I'm not in the mood for this conversation, the same one I've been having with myself for more than a week. "It was temporary for Autumn too. Plus, it doesn't even matter because being single is what's comfortable to me."

Leah slams down her pen with surprising vehemence then proceeds to stomp around my office. "You know what your problem is?"

"I have a problem?"

"Yes, Ren. You do. You have a scarcity mindset. You have trade-off thinking."

I lean back in my chair determined to look casual even if inside it feels as if my nerve endings may actually snap. "Translation, please."

She raises her hands and then slaps them down onto her thighs. "Ren, for somebody who's a legit genius, you can also be ridiculously dense."

"You realize I'm your boss, right?"

"Fuck off, Ren. I'm talking to you as my oldest and dearest friend, as somebody who loves you like a brother. No one cares about your business more than I do. I love my job. I love what you're building. But very few things in life are either-or. Why don't you get that you can be a profit-driven corporate leader *and* help others? That you can be completely devoted to your professional mission and be equally devoted to a *person*?" She pauses, then adds, "To Autumn."

Now I stand, expel air from my lungs, and sort through my emotional haze long enough to respond to Leah, whose level-headedness and good judgment have never, in nearly 20 years, failed to –

In a flash a loud rumble overtakes the sirens outside, the ringing of phones. A jolt underneath me tosses me backward and I have to grab onto the side of my desk to stay upright.

I —

Leah shrieks and darts under the door frame, her fingernails digging into the jamb. "*BIG ONE!*"

I drop to my knees and scramble under the conference desk. Inches away, the window glass wiggles. The earth rolls and lurches. The alarm from the elevator bank blares, sig-naling that the elevator is stuck. Just outside the door, the receptionist screams. I hear high-pitched shrieks from people one floor below us.

Then —

"It's not stopping!" Leah shouts. The jerks and shakes con-tinue.

My framed map of Argentina drops to the ground. Glass shatters. The large video screen mounted to the wall comes loose and clings precariously to the wall.

But my first and only thought is not my home, not my possessions, but Autumn.

Chapter 25

AUTUMN

Branches scratch at my window, waking me. I'm groggy, in that deep haze, familiar because it happens whenever sadness shoves me into a gaping slumber. It's happened before, when old boyfriends have ended it and I'm on my own. Today, my body is leaden as I shift to glance at my clock.

Shit.

The alarm will go off in three minutes.

I roll away, my vision landing on the other side of the bed. The sheets there are still neatly tucked, the pillow full and puffy, a visual reminder that I'm alone.

It's what you wanted, Autumn.

I hate this feeling and always have. I don't want to be by myself. I want this bed to be rumpled not with just any another person's tossing and turning, but with Ren's. I want to smell his smell, a mix of tea tree shampoo and jasmine, to rub off onto my sheets, onto me.

Before, I needed someone, anyone, by my side. It was a position to be filled, to keep me from isolation.

But while the sorrow is the same, this is different.

I miss *Ren*.

I miss his nerdy earnestness, his attentive listening, his probing questions to find out what I'm all about, which helps *me* learn what I'm all about too. With Ren, for the first time ever, I felt seen. I miss the hunger in his eyes whether I'm wearing a grubby t-shirt or a gown. I miss being truly known.

"Dating" Ren served its purpose, allowing me a provisional reprieve from being asked about dating, enabling me to not resume my lifelong pairing pattern. But it also had an opposite effect: the weeks with Ren, feeling whole and complete, were a tease, a glimpse into a level of connection I've never before experienced, didn't even think was possible. Perhaps *that's* what I've been chasing all these years — not simply a romantic replacement for my closeness with Winter. So those weeks with Ren somehow made it all *worse*, made my goal of living life on my own that much harder.

Buzz! Buzz! Buzz!

I slap off the alarm. When I drag myself upright, my head feels too weighty for my neck, my frame.

I shuffle to the bathroom. In the mirror, my eyes are sunken and my skin is matte. I splash cold water on my face, an attempt to wash away my longing, the mistake I made in agreeing to Operation Voltaire in the first place. I scrape a towel up and down my skin and I stare at myself again. My skin is pink, my eyes still hollow.

Summer and I are not identical but for maybe the first time I recognize something of her on my own face: it's how she appeared months ago, right before she met Cole. There was a latent emptiness in her expression. The look has disappeared not just because she fell in love with Cole, but because Summer found herself, found her power working with young kids and diving into a brand new career.

I need to discover who I am too.

Greta tells me I'm so busy taking care of others that I haven't taken care of myself. Isn't insisting on relational solitude the right thing to do? And if so, how long should I insist on being alone? Should I rush it or be patient? If I wait long enough, will anyone match what I experienced, however briefly, with Ren? Or am I trying to force a self- knowledge that will never come no matter how long I wait?

I lumber to the kitchen, press start on the coffeemaker.

There's no class out there on this, no "Five Steps to Being an Individual," no YouTube video about how to separate oneself from fellow triplets.

Greta says that I'm intent on forcing something that doesn't even need to happen. "The stars will do what they do. The planets will do what they do. Just like they've been doing for thousands of years," she said the other day. "Let the Universe show you it's got your back. Plus, there's a Venus star point happening in just a few days. So just lean in to life — it's the right time."

Whatever.

While the coffee brews, I steam almond milk and heat up instant oatmeal. I bring everything to the dining room table. I blow on the first spoonful of oatmeal as steam rises from the lumpy mush and then turn my phone on.

Speak of the devil.

There are no fewer than six texts from Greta, all some variation of "text me as soon as you get up," which I do.

Sitting down?

Yes.

Forgive me for getting into your business. But did some digging. Ren didn't just donate 25K at the spaghetti fundraiser under the name Edward Lewis. In the last few weeks, "Edward Lewis" has donated tens of thousands to every single one of your pet projects. Adult literacy. Organ donation. Homeless advocacy. Yoga for prisoners. Books for inmates. Feral cat spays and neuters. Even that one that distributes ski clothes to underserved kids.

I drop my spoon in the bowl and use two thumbs to scroll through a list of donations to organizations I've worked with over the years, nearly two screens worth. Nearly a quarter million dollars' worth.

Can you believe it, Aut?

I place my phone face down on the table.

Why would he do this? Why wouldn't he tell me?

I'm stunned. Delighted. Heartbroken. Confused.

Was he trying to send me some kind of message? But if that was true, why wouldn't he have used his real name?

I knew soon after meeting Ren that he was more than meets the eye. He's not an arrogant billionaire who exploits or pilfers. While his professional life is his priority, he's not just in it for the money. His millions are the byproduct of his smarts, his excitement about everything that's possible in space. He's not an entitled tech bro oozing privilege — he's a nerd, a Jewish Latino nerd. I saw how kind he is to employees, generous with everyone. But this, as Edward Lewis....

Maybe this is just his version of a final gift, a thank you. Like my handmade map of Lake Lyla. A billionaire's cordial gesture.

Temptation surges through me. I want to call Ren right now and thank him. But Operation Voltaire has an explicit no contact stipulation, *my* rule.

It's all too late.

Before I can fully process what Ren has secretly done, a rumble erupts beneath me.

BOOM.

The floor sways, shifting backward and forward sharply, then rolling like February waves in the lake. I clutch the edge of the table. Across the room, books and vases fall off shelves, my guitar, which was upright on the couch, crashes onto the coffee table with a strumming thud. The box of school supplies I've been collecting to stuff in backpacks for foster kids topples to the floor. Erasers bounce and plastic bags of ballpoint pens skitter.

The earth moving is louder and angrier than the noisiest thunder, more violent than the most frightening airplane turbulence.

Glass breaks in the apartment above me. A neighbor across the hall cries out.

The ground continues brutally shifting. After too many seconds, I force myself out of frozen shock and dive under the table. A piece of ceiling tile crashes onto the table above me.

Is this it, what we've long been warned about? The Big One? The one that destroys?

Chapter 26

REN

"Let's go." I grab Leah's hand.

"Okay, okay, okay, okay, okay, okay, " she intones, breathless and trembling. She grabs her purse.

We step around broken glass from the shattered frames. Just outside my office the receptionist crawls out from under her desk.

I extend my hand to help her up. "Come on, we're going."

On the way to the stairs, we hear shouts and cries from inside the elevator well. People are trapped. Leah shoots me a pained look as we pass.

"It's okay," I tell her. "Security will come for them."

"Tell *them*," Leah says.

She's right, as always.

I position myself in front of the closed elevator doors and cup my hands around my mouth. "You'll be okay," I yell. "Security is coming!"

"It's going to be hours!" Leah whispers, frantic. "People are probably trapped in elevators all over the city!"

The ground rumbles again.

Aftershock.

Before we can figure out where to take cover this time, it's over.

The receptionist whimpers. I squeeze her hand and then pull her to the stairs where we start running down 20 flights. Heavy metal doors open on each floor as people of all kinds join our terrified march: women in pantsuits, coders in t-shirts and jeans. The metal stairs clang with discordant footsteps.

When we reach the third floor, a man using a cane enters the stairwell and wobbles down the first two steps. I look at his companion, a young woman who looks to be a lawyer or an accountant type.

"My client," she mouths.

I instruct the woman to put one of the man's arms over her shoulder while I take his other arm. Together we lift him off the ground, shouldering his weight as we hustle as fast as we can down the last few flights, eager to reach the ground before more inevitable aftershocks, which any Californian will tell you can sometimes be as fierce as the primary quake.

Finally at the lobby, we release the man.

"I've got it from here," her companion says. "My car's on the street and I'll get him home."

One of the building's security officers guides people out of the building. Another is on a walkie-talkie, communicating with the people trapped in elevators.

"Glass outside, people! Watch your step," the building's concierge instructs.

Our receptionist dashes out the front door. Leah fumbles for her phone. "Samantha!" she says.

"She's gotta be okay," I tell her. Now a bookkeeper, Samantha works from home, the top floor of a duplex in the Richmond District.

"My car!" Leah says suddenly, smiling like a miner who just struck gold. "I forgot I left it here, in the building, when we left for New York."

Without word, we dart back into the stairwell, running down two more flights. Even on a normal day, the garage, in the bowels of a big city skyscraper, is spooky. It's worse now, knowing the building rocked and swayed just minutes ago.

Trembling, Leah pulls keys from her purse.

"I got it," I say, grabbing them. I unlock the car and we both get in.

"Shit, it's filthy," Leah says.

That's an understatement. It's downright unhygienic, with wrappers and bottles, receipts and crumbs. It's long been a joke between us: the slob and the germaphobe as best friends, like the set-up for a TV comedy.

We're the first car to reach the exit but the electricity is out so the garage pass sensor and the long barrier arm that's supposed to lift up to let us out aren't working.

I look over at Leah. "I'm gonna buy you a new car," I say, then hit the accelerator and drive right through the wooden arm.

"Jesus," she says with an hysterical cackle that's part laugh, part sob.

Normally I'd shoot down Geary Boulevard to Leah's house, but stoplights are out all over. Instead, I wiggle around parallel side streets of San Francisco's East-West corridor so we hit stop signs instead of lights. Leah snaps on AM radio and we hear reports of the aftermath.

The Cascadia Subduction Zone, a fault that runs 600 miles from Northern California to British Columbia, just off the coast. Richter scale reading: 7.8. Airport runways shut, freeways being blocked off by the minute as experts begin to check for damage on overpasses, which, in previous earthquakes, have collapsed. Sirens ring in a jarring symphony ahead of us, behind us and next to us.

We pass Webster Street then Fillmore, the devastation already apparent. Soft story buildings, those from the 1900's with garages as the first floor, have tilted, some collapsed. Bricks from house facades dot the sidewalks.

"Leah, listen to me. Once we make sure that Samantha is okay and you've had a shot of whiskey, I need you to do some things for me."

"Where are *you* going?"

"I'm taking this car I just busted — that I'm going to replace — and I'm heading up to Lake Lyla."

Even I hadn't known my plan until I speak it out loud.

This quake was big. And the fault is long. Reports place the impact as far north as Portland.

I glance at Leah's gas gauge. It's full, a huge stroke of luck since power outages mean filling gas tanks won't be easy.

"Ren, you can't go anywhere. Didn't you just hear what that reporter said? Freeways will be shutting down. It's not safe."

This steering wheel is thick and the pedals unfamiliar. I'm so used to being driven by Matthew and my own, brand new Prius.

"Didn't you hear me say I'm buying you a new car?"

"Oh, for fuck's sake, Ren. I don't care about my car. I care about *you*. You shouldn't be traveling. I get that you love her, but—"

I whip my head to stare at her. She's known all along. As with most everything, she knew even before I did.

I love Autumn.

It's why, when the ground gave way beneath us, it was Autumn and only Autumn who flashed before my eyes.

"Here's what I need you to do," I continue, ignoring the revelation. "First, check in on all our California employees, including Matthew. Find out who needs help. People whose homes are uninhabitable. Put people into my house. Once the runways open again, use my plane to fly needy people to my other homes."

"*Other people* in your *homes*? Did you hit your head during the quake, Ren? You, who won't even stay in a hotel room without hospital-grade disinfection?"

None of that matters now. "My houses can only shelter a few people. So use whatever resources necessary to help. Get them hotel rooms. The Ritz, the Four Seasons, I don't give a shit. Just help."

The earthquake didn't just shake and jolt the tectonic plates, it has jolted me. For perhaps the first time, I see what I've been guarding jealously – a jet, homes, collections – it's all meaningless.

I pull up to Leah's house on 6th Avenue and together we run inside. Samantha is calmly sweeping up broken dishes. Leah runs to her and I exhale. With the help of Samantha's steadiness and a shot of whiskey, Leah will be able to execute what I've asked her to.

My phone buzzes in my pocket. A text from my grandmother. Thank God she's in Southern California, far south of the Cascadia Subduction Zone. I quickly thumb a message back, letting her know that I'm okay and not to worry.

I pat the pockets of my jeans. I've got Leah's keys and my wallet. I understand in this moment how very little I need in this world.

"Okay, I'm going," I say.

Leah hugs me, silently communicating her reluctant support for what I'm doing. Over her head, Samantha and I make pointed eye contact and I'm certain Leah will be taken care of.

Emergency vehicles of all kinds travel in all directions as I drive west towards Park Presidio Boulevard. Their sirens serve as a soundtrack to my thoughts.

The one place a hundred percent safe from earthquakes? I say to myself in a tone that I imagine comics use when trying out new bits. *Space.*

Space has been my focus since fourth grade. The true-to-life replica of planets that hung from my bedroom ceiling was one of my first maps, a 3-D version of the solar system. Imagining exploring the cosmos for fun, for profit was a distraction for me, an escape from the loneliness of being an only child with loving but preoccupied parents, of being a nerd without many friends. I told myself I loved space, but I see now that maybe loving it so much was my way of protecting myself: loving something that *couldn't* love me back. Space became a wall, shielding me from potential hurt, rejection.

I'm ready to knock down the wall, to make my career *secondary* for once.

I'm ready to make love the center, the sun, the largest star in my universe.

I'm on the bridge now, fog lifting with every inch I travel toward sunny Marin County a mile north. Sail boats bob like apples in the choppy waters. Coast Guard boats are out in force beside me and down below where the Bay meets the Pacific, on guard for tsunamis that often follow big quakes.

My being ready for love, though, is only part of it. Autumn has her priorities, goals I respect. Not only has she devoted herself to helping others, but she's made a worthy commitment to herself, to finding out who she is when she's unattached, to her sister, to a man. I admire it.

With each mile I travel, though, I grow convinced that she can have independence, autonomy. With her abundance mindset, she taught me that — that there's enough love, enough space for everyone. She can be an individual *and* be with me. I see her for who she is — distinct, whole. She's not merely one of two, whether the second is Winter or me or anyone else.

She's one of a kind.

Unlike my father, I'm not a lawyer expertly trained in making persuasive arguments. It may be too late to convince Autumn that we can give up what we've each long thought about ourselves and move forward together. But I'm going to pour every ounce of myself into trying.

A police car approaches in my rear view mirror and I fear the officer will tell me to get off the road. I lighten my touch on the accelerator. Once over the bridge, I take the Sausalito exit. The police car stays on the freeway and I exhale.

I drive surface streets for about two miles through the charming bayside town and then return to the freeway, the police car nowhere in sight.

Thirty minutes later, I hear on the radio that highway patrol shut the Golden Gate Bridge for inspection. I got across just in time. But if I hadn't, I would have swum the distance to get to the other side, to Autumn.

Long-feared pain and rejection may be waiting on the other end of this journey north. But I'm willing to take the risk.

Chapter 27

AUTUMN

"Canned goods over there! Clothing in that corner! Toiletries and blankets here."

I'm at the Inn, a few hours after the earthquake. It's wreaked havoc as far south as San Jose, as far north as Portland. It lasted 92 seconds, one of the longest earthquakes in US history.

After that terrifying minute and a half, when it finally felt safe to crawl out from under my dining room table, I messaged family and friends. A window cracked in Summer and Cole's condo. Greta got a shiner from being tossed into a hanging cabinet in her kitchen. Winter and my brother Colin were both out of town. Everyone texted back except my parents. I called their home number and got an out-of-order buzz. Panicky, I threw on clothes, ready to drive right over there when my dad finally texted that their cell reception was spotty and their power was out but that they were okay.

So instead of heading to their house, I drove into work. The tourism board becomes a hub during fires and earthquakes and storms. These things affect visitors' ability to return home, whether because roads are closed or a tree has fallen on their car or whatever. When I arrived, Noah was already fielding those kinds of calls. So I set about organizing the food and clothing drives that I knew would be helpful from past experience with storms and quakes and fires. Supermarkets might be closed, power restoration might be delayed. Even if things like canned goods won't be needed this time around, we're a better-safe-than-sorry town, a community of do-ers and givers. And until it's clear what *wasn't* needed, people pitch in just in case. One call to the Inn secured a conference room to serve as mission control. I blasted donation needs on social media and then headed to the Inn, where I am now.

Long practiced in handling the aftermath of natural disasters, Lake Lylans are a generous breed and contributions are already coming in. I try not to think about the last time I was here at the Inn — as Ren's date.

Or was it "date"?

The Inn is one of the primary places where we pretended to be a couple so that he wouldn't be bothered during his conference. But the Inn is so much more than that. It's where we yoked our naked bodies. It's where he brought his lips to every inch of my skin, every crevice and slit, every tip, every valley.

"Brand new athletic socks," a woman says, holding up a plastic grocery bag.

I point to the clothing box in the corner. "Thanks so much – they'll go to good use."

Everything collected here will be taken later today to the rec center, the same location as the spaghetti fundraiser, which will serve as a temporary shelter for anyone with busted windows or without electricity. Temps hover around 45 degrees in Lake Lyla in late November so no one can live here with just a tarp covering a window or without heat.

My phone rings.

"Hey, Noah," I answer after plopping a pile of parkas and puffers into a box. I make my voice friendly so he continues to understand that nothing will be weird between us after I declined his date invitation at the winery.

"Just got a call from the rabbi. His wife's an ER doc and says the hospital could use extra blood donations. They're getting car accidents from roads buckling. And people cut by glass."

I wipe my brow with the back of my hand. "Oy."

"The rabbi said we could use the synagogue parking lot as a blood donation center. His wife is sending over a van from the hospital, but they need a coordinator."

"On it."

Amidst the clank of canned goods being dropped into a cylindrical bin, I let the Inn's manager know that I'm heading to the blood drive but will be back later. I give her my phone number in case there are any glitches. I'm secretly thankful I can remove myself from the reminders of Ren and the memories we made here.

Driving down Chestnut Street, I see someone sweeping glass from the sidewalk in front of Chompers. Bernadette is outside Bernie's wearing a down vest and manning a table where she's handing out free cups of coffee. I toot my horn and give her a wave.

I park in the synagogue lot at the same time as the hospital van. As I walk over to the driver, who's also the phlebotomist, rust-colored sparrows fly in a crisscross pattern above me. The phlebotomist explains how to check donors in, the forms required, and how donors should recuperate after the draw.

Because Noah put out a call for donors on social media, six people are already queued to roll up their sleeves. The rabbi meets me in the building's entryway where not long ago I enjoyed apples, honey and challah after the new year service. He's already set up two folding tables in the foyer. I quickly get the first person checked in so the phlebotomist can begin his work.

"Thanks for coming," I say to the first donor in line.

"Always happy to do a mitzvah," he says.

The line moves swiftly, and donors are patient about waiting for the single phlebotomist to call their names. After checking in the eleventh or twelfth person, I'm finally able to pause and organize the paperwork I've completed so far. I gather the pages together with staples and paper clips provided by the synagogue and place the papers into a folder that the phlebotomist will bring back to the hospital along with the bags of blood.

All of the sudden, the synagogue doors burst open with a blast of blustery air, accompanied by the sound of panting, as if someone has run here from a long distance. I look up then blink rapidly because I simply cannot believe what I see.

Ren is in the doorway, hands on his hips, eyes darting left and right, like a cat hyped up on catnip. He's wearing the no-name jeans we bought together at Barnard's.

Instinctively, I rise to my feet, the metal chair I was on squeaks against the marble floor.

When he sees me, his face relaxes. Then he breaks into a broad smile as if it's me he's been looking for all along.

"Autie!" He hurtles toward me, reaching across the table to grasp my upper body. He's never called me Autie before. "Are you okay?"

"Yes, yes, I'm okay. Are you?"

"I am. I am now, at least. I drove right up here. I was worried. I, I—"

I pull away. "Hang on. Take a breath. Sit down." I guide him to my chair and I lean against the table. "You drove hours from San Francisco after an enormous earthquake to see if I was okay? You could have called...."

He shakes his head. "No, it's more than that." He squeezes my wrists and tilts his head to the far corner of the foyer, away from the waiting blood donors. "Can we talk? Over there?"

I nod and we make our way to the secluded corner.

"Autumn, can we be real with each other?"

I nod again, still astonished that Ren is here, back in Lake Lyla, at the synagogue where we first met.

He takes my hands into his. "I mean *really* real with each other. Not Operation Voltaire. Nothing pretend."

A lump forms in my esophagus and I nod a third time.

"I've missed you," he says.

My heart burns and swells. "Missed you too," I whisper.

"Autie, meeting you has changed my life."

I begin to tremble.

What do I want?

The weeks I was "with" Ren were extraordinary. But isn't that similar to how I've felt with other men? Isn't that what I want to live *without* for once?

"The way you spend your time," he continues, "the relationships you have, the work that you do for other people, the roots you have here. I learned from you that when you have love in your life, you have more to give. Yes, our relationship started out as pretend, as a means to a distinct end. But then, for me, it wasn't."

He steps closer, his lips inches from mine. "Autumn, the 'extra' stuff that happened between us wasn't just because of fleeting lust or because of any contractual obligation. It was real to me. It meant something."

I look into his face and spy glimpses of the eager, geeky boy he must have been. And I see something else too. I must have seen it before but never labeled it until now. I see glimpses of the man he will be — the middle-aged dad, the life companion. And *this* is something new, something I've never once seen in past relationships.

Ren continues to stare. He sees the wheels turning in my brain.

Tears threaten to leave my eyes. I fold my lips inside my mouth and then whisper, "It meant something to me too."

"Being with you makes me want to grow old," he says, precisely echoing my own thoughts. "Being with you was never suffocating or overwhelming or too much. In fact, being apart from you has shown me that it wasn't *enough*. I —"

I place my hand on his chest to stop him.

Because I see now how wrong I was about what I want. Ren is not just another man to fill a spot in my life. I don't need Ren like I needed past relationships.

Once I was merely a half. But now I'm whole. Whole all on my own. I'm whole because Ren has helped me crystalize my identity. Our relationship is not one of need. It's a relationship of two equal but distinctly different individuals coming together, two parts interlinking to become not a whole but something greater than the whole.

He continues speaking despite my gesture.

"I know you want to be alone. I respect that so much, Autumn. I do. But you don't need to be alone to find yourself, to differentiate yourself from Winter or from anything. You're your own person. You say you want to know who you are. But I think you already do. Look at you, here, helping. You didn't follow anyone else here. You led the charge, like you always do in these situations. You've already found your individuality, your own passion. And if you don't believe me, I can help you understand. You don't have to give up on any promises to yourself. I will help you fulfill that promise. I want...I want to make this, to make *us* real."

220

A sound escapes me, a honky, indelicate mixture of a sob and a smile. "What do you mean, exactly?"

"I mean, I mean....let me put it this way." He breaks into a huge, confident grin. "Letting a *contract* dictate the terms of our love affair was a 'big mistake. Huge!'"

The sob evaporates and I laugh fully now.

Pretty Woman has become our love language.

"I know my financial status is not something you like. But, Autie, since Operation Voltaire ended, I've been reevaluating, thinking how I can use my career, my company, my resources to do good – just like you do. So I won't get you a showy ring if you don't want one. I'll sell my plane. Anything. I just want to be with you."

I can't believe this is happening. I can't believe that the sorrow, the discombobulation, the emotional malaise I felt when our contract ended — it's over now.

"Autumn," he says, his breath hot in my ear. "You just *get* life. And I want to be with you for the rest of it."

Chapter 28

REN

Steam rising from the mug mesmerizes me as I sit in a cloudy, in-between state, a leaving and an arriving. I'm in Autumn's living room. A breeze slips through a window that's not quite sealed. There's a mess around me: papers and files for Autumn's charity work, piles of school supplies and backpacks that she tells me are for foster children. For the first time in my life, a mess like this, this disorderliness strikes me as cozy rather than discomforting.

It's the day after the earthquake, the morning after I pledged myself to Autumn, professed my deep desire – a desire like none I've ever experienced – to do life alongside her. Not by agreement. Not for show. But for real, forever.

It feels like more than just the new year of our shared heritage. It's a reset, a whole new start, a renewal. It feels as if I've finally exited my old companionless life and entered a portal, a portal into a new existence altogether, a shared existence where Autumn and I can enjoy a life of mutual strength and evolution.

I risked it all by coming back here to Lake Lyla — not only my safety, driving along highways that may not have been safe after a massive rupture along the Cascadia Subduction Zone, but perhaps even more scary, I risked learning that Autumn's feelings were merely passing, an act.

But in a stroke of luck — more luck than I experienced when diving into a professional field that wasn't even real yet, more luck than making a killing on speculative space deals, more luck than landing partnerships with the biggest and brightest in my emerging industry – no, the luck I've had in the last 24 hours eclipses all of that because Autumn said yes. She said that that she, too, felt what I felt, that she, too, doesn't want to spend any more time apart.

"Ah, I see you got the tea I left for you."

I'm shaken from my musings by Autumn, who walks into the dining room freshly showered and ready for another day of pitching in, of giving of herself, of spending her time helping others. Time, I've learned, is our most essential non-renewable resource. Going forward, I'll take my cue from Autumn now that I've seen how rich her life is, billions or not.

She approaches me, fresh-faced and beautiful, wearing jeans cut off at the ankles, white sneakers and a dark orange sweatshirt. She's casual and sexy, so much sexier than any of those women who people have tried to introduce me to in recent years, women who, in my opinion, try too hard, shellacking natural beauty with expensive tennis bracelets or too much makeup. Autumn, in contrast, is real and authentic and that much more gorgeous because of it. She's who she is through and through. As our lives intertwine, I'll prove to her that she's not her identical sister Winter, not merely one of a triplet, that she doesn't need a pairing. I'll show her that I'm her partner because I choose her and only her every day.

Standing next to where I sit, she runs a hand gently over my head and my whole body tingles. She leans into me, and I wrap an arm around her waist. She kisses my forehead. It's a tender gesture, a sincere one, a kiss of comfort and companionship, and it warms me from the inside out.

"Heading into work now. You all good here?"

Lake Lyla survived the quake remarkably well. There was minor damage – mostly windows, some soft-story collapses. But overall, needs at the rec center shelter were far fewer than expected and the blood drive created a surplus of donated blood that the hospital used not just for people who sustained injuries from the quake, but also for routine surgeries.

"Yup, go on ahead," I say.

"Meet up after? Maybe at Bernie's?"

"Perfect."

"What are you going to do today?"

"A mixture of work and personal stuff. I need to check on whether the quake will affect any of our projects going forward. Touch base with Leah. Things like that."

"Got it." She grabs her bag, which is hanging over one of the dining room chairs. She leans down again, this time kissing me on the lips. Her breath is cool and minty and I feel my body respond to being close to her. I want to pull her towards me, to touch her everywhere, to make her quiver and moan, just like we did last night, our first night back together – our first night *truly* together.

But I refrain.

Start as you mean to go on, as my grandmother says.

I want Autumn to know from the very start that I support everything she does, that we will be complements to each other, that no one's career, no matter how lucrative, will override the other.

"See you later at Bernie's," she says.

I watch her walk to the door, the curves of her seat swaying with each step.

By now the steam has stopped rising from the mug and I take a big sip, the spice perfectly complementing the orange flavor.

I open Autumn's laptop, which she said I could use since when I bolted from San Francisco after the quake, I had only my phone, wallet and keys. I log on to email via the cloud and begin answering messages. Leah and I schedule a meeting with a geologist applying for a water extraction device and then talk by phone about endowing a chair in aerospace design at my alma mater. Leah is still shaken from the quake but has learned that our downtown office is structurally sound and we can return there any time. She's housed a few company employees in various homes and condos of mine and forwards me the texts of thanks.

One couple shared a photo of themselves huddled safely on my couch. It's not easy for me to share. I still get a squirrely feeling inside when I see them on my furniture. But I'm ready to change now. It won't be easy, but I'm ditching what Leah calls my scarcity mindset. And I'm taking a cue from Autumn, who's shown me that there's enough good, enough help... enough.

After an hour, I stand, stretch and head to the kitchen to make another cup of tea. As the water boils in the kettle, my phone rings.

"Hey, Kenny."

"Ren, where the hell are you?"

I tuck the phone between my ear and my shoulder as I rip open a tea bag packet. "What do you need, Kenny?"

"Seriously, dude, where are you? We've got the Illinois conference coming up, the deal with Nebular on the table, not to mention the board of directors meeting to prepare for. And have you followed up with that guy from Galaxy Vapor? You know, who you met at the Infinity Symposium?"

"Geez, slow down. I'm in Lake Lyla."

"What the hell are you doing all the way up there? The conference ended weeks ago."

"I—"

"—hold on a second. You're not with *that woman*."

"Again with the President Clinton vibes, Kenny? *That woman* has a name and it's Autumn."

"Whatever. You still dating her?"

"Now you're my mother?" My comment is both sarcastic *and* ironic since my mother never probed much into my personal life, let alone my dating life.

"We talked about this. Anyone you're dating seriously needs to be vetted."

I leave the kitchen and glance around Autumn's living room. I notice that her fake eyeglasses are on the side table next to her guitar. She left the house without wearing them.

"No, Kenny, *you* talked about this. You think I got to where I am by having bad judgment?"

"Look," he says, and beneath his sigh, I hear the sound of keys being punched on his keyboard. "What's her name? Autumn what?"

I run a finger slowly along the frets of Autumn's guitar, producing soft, tuneless sounds. "There's no need for this kind of alarm."

"But what if she's not who she says she is? What if she's got huge debt? How do you know what she wants from you, Ren?"

My body grows cold.

Just like Kenny, it's my nature to distrust motives, to see life as a zero-sum game. With each success I gained, with each million I acquired, I lost something too. I lost meaning in my life. Kenny, too, I realize then, has gotten too hard, too used to life as cut-throat. I slowly exhale.

I'm ready to get it all back.

So I choose to trust. I choose to relinquish that cautious, cynical view of life, to let it die like the oak leaves that have fallen outside and crunched under my feet when Autumn and I carried donations from the Inn's van into the rec center last night.

"Kenny," I begin slowly.

"Yes?" His upbeat tone implies he's certain I've come around, that I'll authorize his plan — demoralizing to both me and to the woman I love — to scan Autumn's background, to distrust my own instincts.

"You're fired."

Chapter 29

AUTUMN

I stop just outside of Bernie's and peek at the outdoor thermometer on the doorframe. Even though robins, bluebirds and finches crossed my path as I walked here from the office, it's the coldest I've felt in many months. Sure enough, the thermometer reveals it's 39 degrees. I've lived in Lake Lyla long enough to know that I will blink and snow will be dusting the ground. Sometimes this time of year, I feel a sadness, a melancholy when fall – "my" season — is ending. But not now. For once, I'm happily anticipating what's to come, as if I'm on the brink of something magnificent. Soon it'll officially become winter and I'm eager for all its trappings: holiday lights and gingerbread cookies, skiing and snowballs, carols and cozy movies.

Inside Bernie's, the fire roars and I smell nutmeg. As always, Bernadette is behind the counter, her blue- and pink-streaked blond hair covered with a green knit cap, experimenting with recipes for the upcoming holidays.

"Hi, Autumn." She puts down a measuring spoon and looks around the cafe, which is sparsely populated at this late afternoon hour. "Hey, can I get your help with something?"

"Of course."

Bernadette wipes her hands on her apron and swings an arm around, motioning me to follow her into the back room. She pulls a tall footstool up to a wall of shelves and steps onto the highest step.

"Just need a little assistance getting these holiday decorations. I can lift it off this high shelf, but then I need to hand it off – don't want to break my neck stepping back down with my hands full."

"Got it."

Bernadette grunts as she moves a few boxes out of the way and then finds what she's looking for: a cube-shaped cardboard box with "HOLIDAYS" scribbled in uneven black handwriting.

"Okay, here we go. Arms up," she says, yanking the box from the shelf. "It's not heavy, just awkward." She lowers it to me.

"Where to?" I say, clutching the box to my body.

"Right there is fine." She juts her chin at an empty spot on the floor next to the shelves.

"Can I peek?"

She nods.

Inside, there are festive green and red garlands, felt candy canes, blue and white bunting with dreidels and Jewish stars as well as a "Happy Kwanza" sign. It's a reminder that the holiday season will soon be in full swing, that soon it'll be Winter's time. Most people love this time of year, especially in Lake Lyla where snowflakes on pine trees and white, twinkly lights adorn the sidewalks of Chestnut Street, giving the town a vibe that's even cozier and merrier than usual. For obvious reasons, this is the time of year that Winter loves most. Her admirable take-charge and assertive (Summer would say bossy) qualities always seem to kick into high gear around the holidays. And this year is no exception. The other day, she revealed that her unorthodox side hustle has recently taken off, thanks to discreet word of mouth. That's fueled her drive to quietly expand it *and* to develop a related program at her real job at the local gym. She's just hoping an upcoming change in management and administration there won't thwart her plans. Winter can be fierce, though, when she sets her mind to something. I can't wait to see if she pulls it off.

I fold the flaps back down over the box I've retrieved for Bernadette, reminding myself to stay present in the late fall, to not dive into the holiday season just yet. "Anything else you need?"

"That's it. Thanks." She leads me back to the cafe counter. "Now, what can I get you?"

I point to the ingredients resting on her work area. "Whatever you're making there looks and smells pretty good."

She shakes her head. "Not ready yet. But as soon as I've perfected the prototype, you'll be the first to try it."

"Always happy to be your taste tester. So until then I guess I'll have a pumpkin spice latte. Decaf."

"Good choice. Pumpkin spice is only around for another week. Anything else?"

"And a maple latte. Also decaf."

"Two decaf lattes coming up. I'll bring them over."

I take a table in the back next to the fire, the one that's become "our" table since it's where Ren and I first drew up Operation Voltaire and where we sat the night of the spaghetti fundraiser. I take a seat, back to the wall, so I can see when Ren arrives. Until then, I take in the others here: tourists, people pecking at their computers, parents with small kids sharing biscotti. I revel in the comfort I get being in a familiar, cozy place while also waiting for Ren, who represents everything that's new and possible in life.

From the speakers on the wall above me, the tune switches from Drake's latest to JLo's "My Love Don't Cost a Thing." I'd never really listened to the lyrics before. But hearing them now, waiting for Ren, I smile to myself. I'm grateful that Ren knows that even if he was "broke," I'd love him just the same. Perhaps it should become "our" song.

My phone rings and I slide it out of my pocket.

"Hi Greta. What's up?"

"Hey, I have a...question." Her tone is halting, hesitant.

"Shoot."

"Remember when we were at the winery? And you introduced me to Noah?"

"Sure," I say, remembering that day, how broken-hearted I felt about Ren, about our moving on, away from each other, our lives forever separate. And now here we are, together for real. And I feel in my bones that it's for forever. Life has a way of surprising us, even when we believe there are no more surprises to be had, when we're convinced that monumental shifts are no longer possible.

"Well, I...I...."

"Spit it out, Gret."

"We ran into each other today at Chompers."

The sides of my mouth curl upwards. I know where this is going.

"And," she continues, "he recognized me from the winery. We chatted for, like, twenty minutes. He's so funny and smart. Anyway, he asked me out. I was planning to upload my profile to Billionaire Rendezvous that very afternoon and I will definitely still do that if you –"

I haven't had a chance to tell Greta that Ren and I have come back together for good. When I checked in on her after the earthquake, it was hours before he trekked all the way back up to Lake Lyla. I can't bear her discomfort any longer.

"Greta," I say, "it's *fine*. It's better than fine, actually. He's an awesome guy. Go out with him!"

I hear her exhale. "Really?"

"Yes, really. I appreciate you checking with me. You're a good friend. You have my blessing." I decide to save my news about Ren for another time so that Greta can bask in her own excitement. I owe her at least that. It was Greta, after all, who found Ren for me in the first place, amidst her study of the stars.

"Thanks, Aut. Who knows what'll happen but—"

"—it's worth finding out." I finish her thought.

The cafe door opens and a woman I recognize from high school comes in. We were on the yearbook committee together. She sees me and walks toward my table.

"Winter?" she says, tilting her head as she approaches.

I'm about to correct her, to explain that I'm Autumn. But before I can open my mouth she corrects herself.

"No, no," she says, shaking her head. "Autumn! Sorry, I see now. Definitely Autumn. How are you?"

"Great," I say. "How about you?"

"All's well. Just popping in for hot cocoa." She rubs her palms together. "Freezing out there!"

"Winter's coming," I confirm.

Bernadette arrives at my table with the lattes.

"Thanks, Bern."

My high school classmate notes the two drinks. Just then, Ren opens the front door. He's wearing khakis and a navy parka, his hair is windblown, his cheeks ruddy. She glances over at him, sees his flirty wave.

"Ah, you've got a new boyfriend."

I can tell from her tone that she means *another* new boyfriend, my serial monogamy having started back in high school.

"Nope," I say, correcting her. "I've got my last boyfriend."

Chapter 30

REN

Just outside Bernie's, I pause and look up at the sky. Late afternoon is turning to early evening and the air is wispy and thin. The sky, the focus of my professional life, is expansive. A quarter moon is slowly emerging, the stars are just becoming visible. Sky is not just where I've made my fortune, but it's where I finally found the life companion I didn't know I needed. Autumn Sky is my future. The breeze circles erratically and I pull a knit hat from my pocket. I take one more look around. The mountains, the trees, the lake – it's all so different from my home in San Francisco, framed by the vast ocean and skyscrapers. But thanks to Autumn, I'm learning to see the duality in life, that it's not an either or, that I can love the big city and this small mountain lake town.

Inside Bernie's, Bernadette is behind the counter, surrounded by syrups and spices. She waves, making me feel – no, *understand* – that I'm part of this community now. After so many decades on my own, it's a novel sensation to feel a part of something bigger.

Autumn is at a back table, the very same table where we first devised our contract on the day we met in person right after Rosh Hashanah services. She's chatting with a woman who says hello when I approach and then disappears. Autumn stands and throws her arms around my neck in greeting. I kiss her on the lips and when I pull away to look at her face, I see the rest of my life.

She's ordered me a maple latte. I take a sip, letting the hot, nutty liquid slide down my throat.

"So," she says eagerly while pulling a notebook out of her bag, "time for a new contract."

"Great minds," I say, removing my tablet and stylus from the interior pocket of my jacket. Our next formal contract after this one, I realize, will be our ketubah, the traditional Jewish wedding contract.

"First, and most importantly," she says, "I'd like to keep our money separate. Always."

I shake my head, worried she's assumed I'd make her sign a prenup. "I'd never ask you to—"

"Billionaire or pauper," she interrupts, "I want to have my own money and want you to have yours. I'm not completely abandoning my plan for independence, for autonomy."

I twirl the stylus around my fingers. My chest blooms with admiration.

If only you could see this, Kenny, you dumb ass.

Someday soon, I'll fill Autumn in about the changes Leah and I are making to the business. We're drafting a mission statement, our first. Instead of jumping at any and all money-making opportunities related to space, we're going to be mission-focused. The current draft of our mission reads: "To accelerate the exploration of sustainable livability, art and commerce in space — causing no unnecessary harm — through innovation and shared ideas and for the benefit of all humanity." As part of that, we're pledging to apply a percentage of revenue toward charitable causes, particularly environmental organizations devoted to undoing any damage our company may have inadvertently already caused.

"Fair enough," I say to Autumn's first contract term.

"Speaking of fair," she says, a strong note of hesitation in her tone, "where will we live?"

"Here, of course."

She breaks into a relieved grin.

"I mean, what's not to love about Lake Lyla?" I say, gesturing around Bernie's with my stylus. "Look at *this* place alone — it's a microcosm of everything I've experienced here. It's comfortable, friendly, welcoming. I'll definitely keep one of my San Francisco condos and my office there for when I have business in the Bay Area. But for the most part, I can work wherever. So let's start looking for a place here."

"Fifty-fifty?"

"Absolutely," I say. "Something else, though."

"Okay." She readies her pen, poised to commemorate the next term of our agreement.

I reach into my coat pocket and pull out a tiny fabric satchel. I place it on the table and push it gently toward Autumn. Her bright brown eyes widen.

"What's this?" she says.

"I know we're already officially engaged so I'm not going to get down on one knee here in Bernie's. But we don't have a ring yet. For the past couple of months, I've been telling my grandmother all about you. She just sent this to me to give to you. It was her engagement ring. If you don't like it, we'll get you something you love. But maybe you can wear this in the meantime."

She slowly undoes the snap on the old fabric satchel and pulls out the antique ring. It's elegant and understated — platinum with three tiny diamonds embedded into the band itself. Nothing raised — sparkly but not flashy.

She slips it onto her left ring finger. She glances up at me, tears pooling in the rims of her eyelids. "It's...perfect."

I clear my throat, hoping to prevent my own tears from falling. "So happy you like it."

She glances down at her hand, twisting the band around and around, her expression one of disbelief and intense fascination. We're quiet for a few moments.

"One more item of note...." I begin.

She pulls her gaze from the ring, which she clearly loves. I now understand what people mean when they say their heart feels as if it may explode.

"I'm in the process of forming a foundation," I continue.

She leans back in her chair, giving me her full attention again.

"The tentative name is the Ward-Lewis Foundation."

She gapes. "For...for *Vivian Ward and Edward Lewis*?"

"Precisely. Proceeds from the sale of all of my homes and offices outside the two I just mentioned will constitute the initial funding of the foundation. Tens of millions to start."

"What will this foundation do, exactly?"

"Aut, because of you, I've learned how much good there is to be done in the world — on both a macro and a micro level. The foundation can take on the largest of causes — greening the earth, funding cancer research — to the smallest, like getting life-changing medication to a single person who otherwise couldn't afford it."

She brings her hands together in a single, silent clap and then clasps them together. "Incredible. I'm excited for you."

"Actually, I'm excited for *you*, Autie," I say, ready to burst, "because I'd like you to run the Ward-Lewis Foundation."

Chapter 31

AUTUMN

My assistant taps lightly on the frame of my open office door. I spin around in the rolling desk chair, a notable improvement from the setup I had at the tourism board. Who knew what a difference ergonomic furniture and a lightning fast computer can make in efficiency?

Zippers runs around in circles at the noise. He's my dog now that Ren and I are getting our own place. Greta says she was holding Zippers for me all along. "I knew you two were meant to be together — just like I knew that about you and Ren."

"Yes?" I say to the knock.

"Your sisters are here," my assistant says.

Before I can even say "send them on in," Summer and Winter barge through the door, Winter – no surprise – leading the way. My assistant raises his eyebrows at the audacity and I giggle.

"No worries," I assure him. "Unless I'm in a meeting, these two are always allowed to come in."

"That's what I tried to tell him," Winter says with a faux wicked look. She's wearing a slouchy red knit hat and looks beautiful. She let the highlights she got in early summer grow out and the darker hues to her hair brighten her face and highlight her cheekbones.

Maybe I should let mine grow out as well.

I've ditched my fake eyeglasses, dropping them in the donate bin at an optometrist office on Chestnut Street. I no longer feel the need to differentiate from Winter in superficial ways. I understand now that though we may look exactly alike, we're each our own people. She's confident and determined. I am quieter, useful. We'll always share a special, otherworldly bond, a connection that only other identical siblings can relate to. But I no longer feel I must force a separation from her. Our lives are on different but parallel tracks. My life path is filled with service, with Ren, all things separate from Winter's.

Summer hangs behind, her thick, wavy hair — which Winter and I have always coveted — swept back in a low ponytail. Her cheeks are pink and plump. She's wearing a bulky overcoat and holding a long rectangular gift wrapped in dark orange paper and topped with a green bow. Those have always been my favorite colors: the colors of autumn.

"So how's life here?" Winter says, roaming around my office, running her hand along the birch table and peeking out my window, which has a lovely view of Chestnut Street and, if you squint, of the Inn.

The Ward-Lewis Foundation set up shop in this office about three weeks ago. Ren and I picked this space because it's nice enough to host potential donors and recipients of our grants, but not so fancy as to pull funds away from our central mission, which we've determined is "to prevent and alleviate the suffering of all beings, and to inspire learning, connection and positive progress."

"So far so good," I say.

Summer approaches my desk. "What'cha working on?"

"Well, right now evaluating grant proposals from organizations that fight hunger, protect coral reefs, ensure safe drinking water, and bring yoga into high schools."

As I tell them more about the proposals, Winter inspects the one personal object I've brought to the office: a framed photo of me and Ren, the selfie we took at Bernie's on Rosh Hashanah, the first day we met in person, the day we hammered out the details of Operation Voltaire. I love the picture because it captures *possibility*. Neither of us had a clue that our lives we're about to change forever. The photo is a powerful reminder that no matter how hard you try to design your life, unexpected, beautiful, glorious surprises are always possible.

"New beginnings for you all around," Winter says.

"Yup," I agree. "New relationship, new job here with the foundation. It's bananas how it so perfectly aligns with my strengths, my goals, my interests."

"I think that's my cue," Summer says, and hands over the gift. "An office-warming present."

The paper crinkles as I unwrap the gift, a wooden sign with the word "wheelhouse" painted in dark orange lettering.

"Because," Summer adds, "this job is squarely within your wheelhouse!"

"This foundation is lucky to have you — helping people is what you're all about. It's not just that this job was made for you — *you* were made for this job," Winter adds.

I throw my arms around my sisters. "Thank you. This means a lot. I'll hang it after our lunch."

"Do you miss the tourism board at all?" Winter asks. "You were there for so long."

"I do. I miss the familiarity of my role. And my colleagues." I think of Noah, who not only has been happily dating Greta for the last several weeks, but also got promoted to the job I left.

I place the Wheelhouse sign on my desk and pull out Zippers's favorite toy to play with while I'm out. "So, where should we go for lunch?"

"Soup," Winter declares. "It's freezing outside! Anywhere I can get a big bowl of hot soup."

Chapter 32

AUTUMN

It's the last Thursday of November, Thanksgiving night. Hanukkah begins in just three days. We're on the walkway leading to my parents' house and noting how uncommon it is for the two holidays to land so close together.

"Glad it happened this year," Ren says, wrapping his arm around me, "so we can celebrate this fortuitous confluence together."

I lean my head against his shoulder, place my arm around his waist. "Me too."

In just the last week, the season has unquestionably shifted from fall to winter. It snowed the last two days, leaving a light dusting on my parents' walkway. The trees in their front yard are officially leafless. The pumpkins that had adorned their front porch have been replaced by a wreath that's half green and red and half blue and white, a nod to our family's interfaith composition.

Ren is carrying a plate of latkes he made using his grandmother's special recipe, a combination of russet potatoes, sweet potatoes and a hint of cumin, his grandmother's nod to his multicultural heritage. I can't wait to taste one. But more than that, I can't wait to meet his grandmother and his parents. We're heading down to San Francisco in ten days, and the three of them will meet us there. I've talked to them on FaceTime. His grandmother is the quintessential "bubbe," energetic and loving. And his parents, while brisk and efficient, fitting the workaholic stereotype he's described, were lovely when we spoke.

The front door is unlocked and we let ourselves in. Instantly I smell cocoa and peppermint, which means my mom is making peppermint brownies, her signature dessert this time of year. There's also the sharp aroma of grilled onions and shallots from my dad's famous Thanksgiving stuffing. He makes it just how I like: not too mushy, not too crunchy.

We spot my dad at the kitchen table queuing up his famous holiday playlist, with hits from Mariah Carey, Barbra Streisand and Nat King Cole, among others. Seeing us arrive, my mom pauses her chopping to rush over and greet us with tender hugs. She's wearing a punny apron that says "I love you a latke." We've had a few meals here in recent weeks, and it's clear my family adores Ren. He and my dad geek out about telescopes, and my mom, in typical Jewish mom fashion, probes indelicately about when the next Sky family wedding will take place.

I'm getting more and more comfortable with Ren's life, the maps strewn about the house, the intense conference calls I overhear. And he's eagerly diving in to mine, loving the more relaxed, casual pace of mountain life. He even got his own used guitar and we've begun teaching ourselves U2's One.

"How can I help?" I ask my mom.

"Autie's perennial question," she says to Ren with a wink, then leads me to the counter where she sets me up chopping bell peppers for salad. Ren joins Winter, who's working on a jigsaw puzzle with our new brother-in-law Cole. Our younger brother Colin, who's finishing his college semester in Chicago, will be home in a few weeks just in time for Christmas.

Summer is decorating the table with gourds, dreidels, and gelt, the chocolate Hanukkah coins. She looks plumper than she did at our lunch just a few days ago. I have my suspicions but won't ask. Perhaps tonight she'll reveal some happy news of her own.

As I plop a handful of diced peppers into the salad bowl, the music shifts to Madonna's version of Santa Baby, and I hear snippets of a conversation about the upcoming Snow Spectacle, Lake Lyla's ski festival. It's the town's official welcoming of winter, complete with concerts, fireworks and a snowy mountain party, accessible by gondola, atop the highest ski slope.

With the sounds of family surrounding me, the smell of stuffing baking in the oven and the sizzle of latkes frying on the stove, I pause my chopping, overwhelmed with the just-right way my life has unfolded in only a few months. It all started with Greta and Leah, our two dearest friends, matching us on a crazy billionaire dating site without our knowledge, against our will even. Somehow it morphed into a contract that served our mutual desire to stave off real relationships. That agreement represented old versions of ourselves, versions centered on fear and alienation. But through that bogus contract we somehow created a real relationship, one based on passion and courage and connectedness. I've broken from my co-dependent past. I'm ready to move forward, to share a life of *inter*dependence with Ren, the man who's shown me how unique I really am.

We still have things to work through. We come to our partnership with different emotional scars, different goals. But we're working through them together. Our new home — in my hometown but with his sleek, modern design sensibility — is a perfect illustration of that.

Resuming my chopping, I tilt my head and glance over at Ren, my fiancé, my future, and see that he's been staring at me this whole time. He smiles, that beautiful smile that lights up his whole handsome face, and I see in him our own individual evolutions, our combined future. I grin back at him, wordlessly conveying how excited I am to be here with him, to see how we each continue growing together.

More Lake Lyla
Romances

Summer steers clear of relationships due to her disastrous dating past, at most allowing herself the occasional fling. But her peaceful, predictable life is upended by Lake Lyla's newest resident, Cole, a former Marine and single dad jilted by his ex-wife.

Cole vows that his one and only priority is stability for his daughter. The last thing he needs is to be derailed by Summer, his daughter's soccer coach, who can't hide her sexiness with baggy sweatshirts and blue hair dye.

Everything changes when Summer shows Cole the wonders of Lake Lyla, her family's home for generations. They form a fierce, undeniable connection that neither of them wants.

Peppered with fun banter, secrets and long-held angst, Summer Sky is the first in the Lake Lyla series – a potent reminder that letting yourself believe in love may be life's hardest, and most rewarding, choice. Available on Amazon and Kindle Unlimited.

Likeable, take-charge Winter has never been one to back down from a challenge. For Owen, maintaining the emotional walls he's spent years building isn't easy when Winter's joyful manner is a force as strong as a December blizzard.

Tension builds as Winter and Owen are forced to spend time together, reaching a breaking point as sexy sparks fly.

The third in the Lake Lyla series, Winter Sky is sure to warm your heart for the holidays. Available on Amazon and Kindle Unlimited.

Sneak Peek: The First Two Chapters of Summer Sky

Chapter 1 – SUMMER

"No way."

I'm on the phone with my best friend Jules, who is trying to set me up — again. But I'm not having it.

"He's in town for a conference, staying at The Inn. He stopped into the store. Super cute. Medium height, reddish hair. I –"

"Nope."

I'm a *little* curious but I'm not going to tell Jules that. I don't want a boyfriend – I've learned from my sisters and from what happened with Jordan that I'm just not meant to have Relationships with a capital R. I'm not opposed to an occasional fling. I *am* in my twenties. I have needs, after all. But the flings I have every once in a great while meet distinct criteria: short, sweet, no strings. At the beginning of a fling, I have the end in sight.

"When was the last time you –"

"—'member that guy? The music producer in town for a few weeks for the Boogie Oasis concert?"

He was a nice guy – attentive, interesting, a great kisser. He called me a few times in the weeks after he left town, but I let him know (kindly, of course) that what was done was done.

"That was last summer!"

"So?" I say.

"So in case you haven't noticed, it's *June*!"

Of course, I'd noticed. Lake Lyla has been bathed in glorious, robust sunshine in recent weeks. The smell of pine peppers the air. Brilliant zinnias and begonias are arriving daily at Leaves & Petals, the garden center where I work.

"Work's been crazy," I say. "Fuchsia and daisies to plant, verbena plants to pot and... things to be done. No time."

Jules sighs. "You've had the same job since college breaks, Summer. There's nothing you can't do there with your eyes closed, your hands tied behind your back and within your allotted work hours."

"I'm busy caring for my new rescue cat!" I offer. But I can't fool Jules. She knows the cat barely acknowledges me even though I spent untold sums and many weeks nursing her from a pathetic, bag-of-bones, mangy feline into a plump, energetic cat with a shiny calico coat.

"You've been busy avoiding life!" Her words are harsh but her tone is softening.

"Not true. I've been prepping for my new coaching gig!"

In fact, I'm in the car on my way from Leaves & Petals to Lansberg Field for the first game as soccer coach to a group of 11-year-old girls. Most of them are newbies, which is good because I haven't played since I was a teenager. I spent all spring taking online courses on soccer, learning offensive techniques, how to teach dribbling drills. And I also independently studied coaching strategies – how to instill confidence in pre-teen girls and other social-emotional skills I didn't learn at their age.

Jules exhales loudly, signaling that she finally accepts my hard no on the blind date.

At a stop light I grab a baby wipe from the side pocket of the driver's side door and rub it around my cuticles. I love working at Leaves & Petals. It's both familiar and ever-changing, from the wintergreen boxwood to the daffodils. Working there is grounding, keeping me connected to the earth. But the occupational hazard is that I'm always covered in dirt and sometimes smell like soil. While I'm not interested in attracting a boyfriend, brown gunk under fingernails isn't a good look for anyone. I push the wipe under my fingernails, run it around all ten of my ring-covered fingers.

"What happened with Jordan was not your fault," Jules says.

I crush the baby wipe in a fist and throw it onto the floor. When will Jules – and everyone else – accept what I learned from Jordan and from my relationship with my sisters?

I'm simply not meant to be coupled.

I don't fight my solitary lot in life, even if I do feel a stab of pain now and then when I'm with my sisters or observing newly engaged couples who come into the garden center shopping for wedding centerpieces. It must be wonderful to be wholly connected and...understood. But I accept my fate, which was established at my atypical birth and confirmed after Jordan. I mean, people have *real* problems like food insecurity and chronic illness. I'm content just staying in my lane, working at the garden center and taking advantage of everything Lake Lyla has to offer all year round. If I'm honest, though, I occasionally wonder what else I could do, beyond my job at Leaves & Petals, which is how I ended up with this new coaching side hustle.

"You need to get out of your comfort zone." Jules resumes her frequent refrain.

"I *am* getting outside of my comfort zone! I'm on my way to my first soccer game *as coach*." I don't mention that I'm a nervous wreck. Coaching pre-teen girls soccer, teaching them to be bold, to use their voices, to have self-esteem – that's *way* out of my wheelhouse, something Jules, who's known me since we were kids, should know.

"We're not done with this conversation but I've got to go – a huge shipment of the latest Colleen Hoover book came in this morning and we're expecting a rush of customers in the next few hours." Jules runs The Book Mark, one of Lake Lyla's beloved institutions. It's part book store, part cafe and one of my favorite places on earth. "Want to come by the store later?"

"As appealing as it sounds to continue being badgered by you," I quip, "this first game is going to drain my social battery. But save me a copy of the new Colleen Hoover?"

"Already did."

Driving down Chestnut Street, I pass Swirls, the ice cream shop, and Dubin's, a kayak store in the summer and ski shop in the winter. On my right, Lake Lyla shines like a sapphire, its surface shimmering with white sparkles in the afternoon sun. Lake Lyla – the lake and the town – were named for my great-great-great grandmother Lyla Lansberg, who, according to family lore, was a bawdy, extra-loving feminist who lobbied for women's suffrage and civil rights, and married a much younger man. Many of her descendants, like me, still live in this stunning town on the north shore of the California lake, less than an hour from both Oregon to the north and Nevada to the east. My family's deep history with the area and the many relatives who live here are just two of the nearly uncountable reasons I love Lake Lyla.

"I'm passing Morgan Point," I tell Jules. "This view...it just never gets old."

"Yeah, but *you* are, Summer Sky."

"Need I remind you, Jules, that you and I are the same age?" Barely more than a quarter century.

I turn left onto a narrow lane that will take me to Lansberg Field. I lower my window to inhale the scent. My sisters and I have a nickname for this smell, a pleasing, nearly indescribable combination of pine and eucalyptus, plus the nostril-cleansing properties of some of the freshest air in California. We call it SLS, which stands for "smells like summer." I make a mental note to text my sisters before I get out of the car.

"I'm almost at the pitch," I add, pulling into the parking lot. "Anything else you'd like to berate me about?"

"Mmm..." she says with a faux pensive tone. "Oh, yes, one more thing: what are you wearing?"

Damn. She got me.

I glance down at my athletic shorts – the polyester ones with a wide navy stripe, the ones that hit me at my knees. They're deliberately unflattering. I can't tell her about the shorts or the straight-sided, mismatching tank I'm also wearing. Or the just-in-case purple sweatshirt I'll be tying around my waist. It's my standard *just-move-along-nothing-to-see-here* outfit.

"That bad, huh?" Jules says in response to my guilty silence. "Summer! What if there's some hot guy ref'ing the game?"

Exactly.

"Gotta run. Love ya, Jules!"

I park, text "SLS!" to my sisters, who both immediately respond with thumbs up, and gather my unruly thick hair into a ponytail. I spy through my windshield my team of girls waiting for me. I've only been coaching them a week but already they're a fun, confusing, hilarious and frustrating group. They seem at once too old and too young to be eleven, sometimes sassing like 16-year-olds, sometimes bursting into tears like toddlers. I've been teaching them the basics of soccer as well as the value of supportive teamwork. During our twice-weekly practices, we focus more on passing than scoring, more on encouraging each other and trusting ourselves than achievement. It's the kind of values-based sports I wish I'd been exposed to as a kid. But I have zero sense of how this approach will play out in an actual game.

A few girls run up to me when they spot me getting out of the car. Others stay back, either too cool or too shy to show emotion toward their rookie coach. I return hugs and hand my bag of balls and other supplies to Livvy, a curly-headed player who recently moved to Lake Lyla. As I walk with her and the other girls toward the field, I avoid the crowd of parents chatting nearby, some clearly watching us from the corners of their eyes. This is what I meant when I told Jules that coaching soccer is way out of my comfort zone. I'm not big on crowds or being the center of attention – that's my sisters' domain.

I swallow, keeping my eyes downcast as the girls and I dump our supplies and set up a practice area on the sidelines.

"Summer, look at this!" says a teeny firecracker of a girl with shiny blond hair, the kind of kid who would have intimidated the hell out of me when I was in sixth grade. She dribbles the black and white ball on top of her alternating bent knees.

"Excellent," I say. "I can see you've been practicing. How about you show the others how you taught yourself to master that trick?" She nods with serious conviction as her team-mates gather around.

The other team – from the south shore of Lake Lyla – arrives in two white vans. When they reach the field, I introduce myself to the coach and high five some of his players and wish them a good game. Then I head back to the sideline to give my first-ever pre-game pep talk.

"Alright, Lake Lyla Lady Lions! Are you ready to put into action what we've been practicing? Eye on your target, strive to be the first to the ball, share the glory."

The girls jump up and down with excitement, ready to dart onto the field.

"I love your enthusiasm! Just one more thing: you've earned the right to be here. You're prepared and you're strong."

Here goes nothing.

The first half goes well. We score in the first few minutes and display impressive defense. Some tears are shed when one girl misses a penalty shot and another accidentally caught the ball with her hands instead of blocking it with the top of her head. But overall I'm pleased that the girls seem to be internalizing the rules and strategy of the game. Once they're off the field, I ask their opinions about what they've done well and what they think we should do differently in the second half.

"Peaches for everyone!" the snack mom declares. While sliced oranges are the snack of choice during winter soccer, sweet and juicy stone fruits are abundant at Lake Lyla in June. The girls squeal and shove their hands into a metal bowl filled with yellow and pink peach slices.

My shoulders twitch reflexively when the ref's whistle blows.

The second half begins well but with a few minutes left, we're tied 1-1. I make a shift in the lineup, bringing in some of the weaker, less confident players, and pulling out a few of my strongest players, including curly-haired Livvy. This will surely result in our loss, and I'm nervous about how the parents will react. Indeed, as soon as I make the switch, a few moms and dads furrow their brows and huddle together, gossiping in confusion. I struggle to ignore my pounding heart, to not be intimidated. After all, this is precisely why I wanted this side hustle – to give girls real-world lessons about what's important.

Livvy and the other players jog off the field, red-faced from running in the afternoon heat. A few look disappointed and the girls I'm bringing into the game seem confused.

"Alright! We've got a few minutes left in our first game and I'm excited to see where it'll go. I have confidence in you," I say.

But not surprisingly the Lake Lyla Lady Lions lose after our subbed-in goalkeeper misses an easy block in the last moments of the game. But at least it wasn't a total blowout.

I cheer wildly for the other team as all the players exchange obligatory sweaty handshakes.

"Great job, South Shore," I say, clapping loudly. "I enjoyed watching you play. We look forward to our second match-up later this season."

Back on our sideline, I gather my team and tell them how proud I am of their first game. To the annoyance of some of the parents, who are apparently eager to head out, we huddle together in a tight circle for post-game appreciations.

"I'll start," I say. "I appreciate how Maddie offered Kira a hand when she tripped."

"I appreciate how Sarah said 'good try' when I missed a goal."

"I appreciate how Ella's mom gave me a ride to the game."

After the appreciations, I dismiss the players, eager to end the *let's-get-a-move-on* stares from some parents and to collapse on my couch. How can Jules insist I should have a boyfriend? Even a short-term fling seems emotionally exhausting at this moment.

"Interesting substitutions." A low, husky voice from behind startles me.

I whip around to see Livvy, holding hands with a man I assume is her father, a man who is, um, gorgeous. A few inches taller than me, dark hair, even darker eyes, sexy five-o'clock shadow, full lips.

God, those lips.

My flesh heats from the inside, my belly flip-flops. Why did Jules have to remind me that my last fling was an entire *year* ago?

Flustered by my body's reaction to this man, I lean down and toss soccer balls into the netted bag. Livvy lets go of her father's hand to assist me.

"The girls sure did great for their first game," I say, avoiding his critique about substitutions.

"Probably would have won if you kept certain girls in." He gives me a pointed sideways glance toward Livvy, who's cinching the ball bag shut.

My heart creeps up into my throat. Exposing myself to this kind of judgment is why coaching is so unnerving. I like keeping to myself. But it's also why I'm doing it: Livvy and the other Lady Lions need to learn to rebound from loss and frustration, things I wish I'd learned.

I look into the man's eyes, the color of black coffee, so dark his pupils are indistinguishable from the irises.

"Team sports are about more than winning," I reply softly. *God, how corny.*

"Yeah, Dad. We got great exercise. See my muscles?" Livvy extends her right arm to the side and then bends at the elbow.

He gives her bicep a squeeze and then brings his plump lips to the top of his daughter's head.

Silently, my breath lurches.

Livvy hands me the bag of balls and follows her dad, who's already making his way toward the parking lot. She gives me a wave. "See you next practice, Coach Summer!"

————-

Chapter 2 – COLE

"Should we do Hannah Van Buren or Julia Grant?" Livvy asks.

We're in the cocoon of my car, a cozy place I love to be with her. We're driving home from her first soccer game, one in which she displayed terrific athletic promise, if I do say so myself. Her dribbling was coordinated, her sense of field position impressive.

"Wait, never mind," she says. "Let's repeat Louisa Adams! She's one of my faves. Remember she's the first First Lady to be born and raised outside the US?"

Livvy and I have been listening to the Fabulous First Ladies biography on audio whenever we're in the car together. It's about all the First Ladies, from Martha to Jill, complete with original sources like letters and of-the-day newspaper reports, as well as engaging narration. We skip around, listening to the biographies out of order, sometimes repeating ones we like before moving on. We both find the women captivating, way more interesting than their more famous husbands.

"I remember," I say, handing her a chocolate milk, her favorite snack. I open one for myself too and exhale after a long, cold cocoa sip. Thick, enveloping air drifts into the car through the open sunroof, bringing with it a delicious, evergreen smell I never experienced before moving to Lake Lyla.

I arrived here barely a month ago, just a few weeks after Livvy and her mom, my ex. That's where we're headed now – it's Stacy's night with Livvy. I wish I could just keep my daughter swaddled with me in the car learning about First Ladies and drinking chocolate milk.

Stacy and I get along well enough considering what happened between us. I do have to hand it to her for bringing us both here to Lake Lyla where she landed a great job in hospitality at the Moonlight Peak Inn & Resort, which, I've learned, is referred to as simply "The Inn" by locals. It was hard to leave Cincinnati, where we'd been living since I was discharged from the Marines not long before Livvy was born. Our life as a family had been there. My friends were there.

But Lake Lyla was where Livvy would be and nothing matters more to me than Livvy. The town has turned out to be a hidden jewel, a one-of-a-kind respite from city life, with kick-ass mountain scenery and a small-town sensibility. Most importantly, Livvy seems happy here already.

I stayed in Cincinnati a few weeks longer, wrapping up the sale of my house and preparing to move my one-man consulting business to California. I regret not getting here early enough to coach her soccer team myself, if parent coaching is even a thing in this community. As it is, that woman Summer made some questionable choices in today's game. After Livvy proved adept at ball handling and another player scored a terrific goal, she pulled out those two and other strong players, subbing in girls who are still figuring out the rules of the game and how to maneuver the ball with their insoles. It was an unquestionably odd call considering the Lady Lions could have won otherwise.

"What'd you think of the game?" I ask Livvy, keeping my tone neutral.

"Fun." She takes a long, loud slurp of her drink and wipes the excess brown liquid from her lips with the back of her hand.

"What'd you think of your coach?"

I don't reveal that what *I* noticed about her coach is that she has shapely legs that she couldn't hide with long, baggy athletic shorts. And her wavy hair was sexy as hell, even held back in a low ponytail, with alluring wisps escaping and framing her face. When she lifted her hand to shade her eyes as she spoke to the team after the game, I noticed her fingers were adorned with multiple rings. And when I asked her pointedly about the seemingly incomprehensible substitutions, she twisted one ring in particular around and around below her knuckle.

"I like that she asks us what we think."

"Mmm." *They're eleven*, I think. "How'd you feel when she subbed you out?"

Livvy gulps the last bits of her drink. "Didn't mind. I was kind of tired from all that running. And Rosie hadn't had a chance to play yet." With both hands, she squishes the box of milk and accompanies the move with a grunt. "Can you turn on Louisa Adams?"

I maneuver down Chestnut Street, a beautiful tree-lined street that hugs the shore of Lake Lyla. I slow down, partly to prolong my time with Livvy before dropping her at Stacy's and partly to avoid large ruts in the road, remnants of the vehicle tire chains from Lake Lyla's legendary ski season a few months ago.

Wanting a smooth ride is perhaps an apt metaphor for the life I'm working to create for Livvy. I, too, am an only child and the product of divorce. I know from painful experience that it can be rough, filled with confusion, guilt, instability and loneliness. And in my case, it involved the complete absence of a father figure – my parents split because my dad just kept leaving, eventually disappearing for good – and a revolving door of men coming into our lives as my mother dated all throughout my teen years. My mother's relationships were plentiful, as well as intense and short-lived.

I'm determined that Livvy have an easier time than I did. If it were up to me, there would have been no divorce. But once Stacy cheated, she left me no choice. My first nights away from Livvy as joint custody began were agony. I missed her so much it was physically painful. And it forced me to return to a traumatic time in my own life that I longed to forget.

Making life easier for Livvy than it was for me is why I followed Stacy to Lake Lyla instead of insisting that she stay in Ohio, which I would have been entitled to do per our divorce agreement. Livvy's emotional well-being is also the reason I grit my teeth and force myself to be pleasant to both Stacy and Brent, her live-in fiancé, the man she cheated with.

"For God's sake, Cole," I hear my mom's sharp voice in my head as Livvy is enraptured listening to Louisa Adams's role in the Treaty of Ghent. "I don't care what that dumb mess of a saying is — you don't *really* think history repeats itself, do you? Livvy's experience is Livvy's, not yours."

My mother, who gave up dating altogether around the time that Stacy and I married, is cranky and blunt and often short with me. But she's also the wisest, funniest and most loving person I've ever known. Though she's long been eligible to retire from her job as a high school teacher, she continues teaching biology, maintaining her reputation as the "Bio Boss." One of my biggest joys is that Livvy loves her as much as I do, instinctively understanding from a young age that my mother's very noisy bark is far worse than her bite, which is non-existent. Livvy and "Gammy" FaceTime just about every day. They talk about their favorite shows, play word games together and, I know for a fact, sometimes talk about me. I overhear them joking about how overprotective I am or stuck like mud in the past.

Looking back, I probably wasn't the most attentive husband. While it's no excuse, we were so young, just out of college when we met, and I was often gone while serving in the Marines. Still...cheating?

Rather than take out my anger and heartbreak on Stacy and Brent, I let out my aggression on my skateboard, practicing fakies, switches and heelflips until my legs wobble.

"When's that daddy of yours gonna wake up and realize he's not a pimply twelve-year-old? He needs to give up that darn skateboard already!" my mom regularly laments to Livvy.

I can't help but wonder what my mother would think about Livvy's coach, Summer, about how she most certainly knew she'd be losing the Lady Lions' first game by putting in that cockamamie lineup at the end. My mother would undoubtedly razz me for being too invested in a soccer game for 11-year-olds.

"Oh, get yourself a damn life, Cole," she'd probably say.

Inwardly, I roll my eyes in reply to this imagined conversation. She should know by now that nothing matters more to me than my daughter's happiness, even if that means I can be a little too...involved.

I sneak a peek over to Livvy now, her brow crinkled in rapt interest as she listens to descriptions of Louisa Adams, who led what the biographer describes as "a full and charmed life."

We're now on Rampart Street, just moments away from Stacy's house.

That's what I want for you, Livvy. I think. *A full and charmed life.*

Read Summer and Cole's story on Amazon and Kindle Unlimited.

The author of flirty, fun, fast feels, Jenna Starly is the pen name of women's fiction writer Erin Gordon. Learn more at JennaStarly.com.

Get your free, exclusive guide to Lake Lyla: visit JennaStarly.com.

Readers, You Have Power!

Word of mouth means so much to the success of a book. Readers, you have power! If you enjoyed Summer Sky, please leave a review at Amazon, Goodreads or BookBub — and tell your romance-loving friends!

Printed in Great Britain
by Amazon